One For Sorrow

Philip Caveney

Published by Fledgling Press 2015

Cover Design: Kylie Tesdale
lalliusmaximus.wix.com/kylietesdale

Printed and bound by:
MBM Print SCS Ltd, Glasgow

ISBN: 9781905916955

MIX
Paper from
responsible sources
FSC® C117931

This book is for the nicest in-laws a fellow ever could
hope to have.
Jon, Frances, Dylan and Esme . . .
thanks for everything.

Foreword

Robert Louis Stevenson's classic novel *Treasure Island* started life in a children's magazine called *Young Folks*. It was published in a series of weekly instalments between 1881 and 1882. Stevenson's original title for the story was *The Sea Cook*, but it rejoiced under several long and unwieldy titles along the way; and he chose to publish the adventure under the pen name of Captain George North, because he didn't feel it was 'serious literature'.

It wasn't until May 1883 that it was finally released as a book with the title that we all know and love. It has remained in print ever since, has inspired countless other pirate books and films and is recognised as one of the greatest 'coming of age' novels ever written. How Stevenson came to decide that it might have a life beyond its humble origins has been a matter of debate ever since.

What historians do not know, is that Stevenson had some help on the matter . . .

This is the story of a boy from the future who travelled back in time to offer his advice and inspiration, not just for *Treasure Island*, but for some of Stevenson's other classic works.

One

It was something to do with the magpie. Tom only came to that conclusion long after the event, but the moment he saw the bird sitting calmly on the motorway barrier in the glare of the car's headlights, he knew that it was the start of something; that it was all going to happen to him again and that there was nothing he could do to stop it.

Everything had been going so well, up to that point.

Mind you, it hadn't started promisingly. He remembered coming home from his school in Manchester, one afternoon in mid-December, to find Dad and his new partner, Ruth, sitting on the sofa, looking decidedly shifty. Ruth was a primary school teacher and Tom liked her, he really did, the two of them got along just fine. She tended to come across as meek and mild, but she could wrap Dad around her little finger when she put her mind to it. Tom was listening to his favourite band, The Deceivers, on his iPod as he walked in. He was planning to grab a bit of toast and head up to his room to play on his Xbox, but Dad had clearly been waiting for him to get back from school.

He gestured for Tom to take out the earphones. 'Can I have a quick word?'

'Sure.' Tom switched off the music and stood there, his school bag still over his shoulder. He noticed that Ruth was gazing abstractedly out of the window, sort of trying to pretend she wasn't there, but fooling nobody.

Dad looked very serious. 'Ruth and me, we were just talking about our plans for Christmas,' he said.

'Oh, yeah?'

'Hmm. We've, well, we've booked a cottage in Derbyshire, for Christmas and New Year. A little place, way out in the sticks . . .'

'Will there be WiFi?' This was always Tom's first thought in situations like this. 'Only, it sucks when I can't get in touch with my mates, so . . .'

Something in Dad's guilty expression made him tail off.

'Er, no, Tom, you don't understand.' Dad looked flustered. 'Me and Ruth are going to Derbyshire. Just the two of us. We, er . . . we didn't really think it was your kind of thing.'

The truth hit Tom like a punch to the stomach. They'd never even considered taking him along. They wanted time *away* from him, so they could be all lovey-dovey without him cramping their style. He tried not to look crushed. 'Oh . . . well, that's . . . that's OK, I suppose.

I . . . I can always stay at Jonno's place or . . .'

Dad was shaking his head. 'We discussed this, me and Ruth . . . and we thought, well, what a perfect opportunity for you to head up to Edinburgh and reconnect with your mum. It *has* been quite a while. So, I phoned her and she *loves* the idea. Really looking forward to it.'

'Wait.' Tom actually lifted a hand as if to halt an oncoming vehicle. 'Edinburgh? Dad, you *do* know things always happen to me when . . .'

'It'll be great.' Dad was rushing on, oblivious to Tom's concerns. 'I know you've had a couple of little er, mishaps when you've been up there, but . . . what are the chances of it happening a third time, eh? And you'll be able to stay on for Hogmanay, it's supposed to be a blast!'

'Yeah, but you don't understand. What about Hamish?' Hamish was Mum's new partner and he wasn't anything like as easy to get on with as Ruth.

'What about him?'

'We . . . we don't really hit it off.'

Dad gave him a disparaging look. 'Why not?' he asked.

Tom considered how he might truthfully answer the question. *'Well, you see, Dad, every now and then I go back in time. I never really know when it's going to happen, but it's always when I'm in Edinburgh.'*

'Right . . .'

'And the first time it happened, it was the year 1645 and Hamish was the absolute double of this guy called William McSweeny, a crook who was pretending to be a Dr Rae, a famous plague doctor.'

'I see . . .'

'And after that he chased me back through time to the year 1824, when I was a guest at this lodging house owned by Burke and Hare. You know, the famous serial killers?'

'Uh huh . . .'

'And, the last time I saw McSweeny, he was dissolving in this big barrel of quicklime, so chances are he's dead now, but, well, with him, you can never really be sure.'

Of course, he couldn't say *any* of that. After a lengthy pause, he could only think of one complaint to make about Hamish.

'He's a Hibs supporter.'

'A what?'

'It's a football team.'

Dad looked baffled. 'Well, Tom, it's not as if you're keen on football, is it?'

'No, but . . .'

'So I really don't see what all the fuss is about. You'll have a great time. And Hogmanay in Edinburgh is supposed to be absolutely amazing!'

It was pointless to say anything else unless he wanted Dad to worry about his sanity, so Tom just shrugged his shoulders and quietly accepted his fate.

The week before Christmas he boarded the train at Manchester Piccadilly, waved off by Dad and Ruth, who he imagined would be opening a bottle of champagne just as soon as he was out of sight. But they did present him with a book-sized package wrapped in festive paper.

'This is your main Christmas present,' said Dad. 'We'll give you the other bits and pieces when we see you in the New Year.'

'Don't open it until Christmas Day,' Ruth reminded him. And she gave him a polite peck on the cheek to send him on his way.

But he quickly got bored on the train and unwrapped the present anyway. It was a Kindle. At first he felt a wave of disappointment. He'd never been that big a reader, to be honest, though since discovering that Catriona McCallum had published some books, he'd made an effort to change his ways. He knew that, once again, this was Ruth's influence. She had some kind of bee in her bonnet about him not reading enough books and she'd obviously talked Dad into getting this instead of the computer games Tom had asked for. He switched on the device, which he was glad to see was already fully powered and once he'd experimented with the controls, he discovered that it came pre-loaded with some classic adventure stories. One of them was *Treasure Island*, a book he'd always meant to read, but had never quite got around to. So he grudgingly started with chapter one and within the space of a few pages he was hooked.

He was vaguely surprised when, a little over three hours later, the train pulled into Waverley station, where Mum and Hamish were waiting for him.

This was when things got really weird, because it quickly became apparent that Hamish had changed his attitude. Tom wasn't sure if it was anything to do with the little pep talk the two of them had shared in the National Museum of Scotland, but whatever had happened, it was a leaner, friendlier Hamish who led him to the car and drove him and Mum back to the house in Fairmilehead. On the way, Mum sang Hamish's praises as though she'd become his manager or something.

'Don't you think Hamish is looking good, Tom? He's lost a stone and a half *and* he's going to the gym twice a week.'

'Go, Hamish,' muttered Tom under his breath, but Mum didn't seem to notice. Tom reached into his shoulder bag and pulled out the Kindle, eager to find out what happened next.

Hamish studied him for a moment in the rear view mirror. 'Is that one of those e-reader things?' he asked.

Tom nodded.

'I like the feel of a real book myself. So, what are you reading?'

'*Treasure Island.*' He waited for the inevitable put-down, some line about how Tom needed to get out in the fresh air, do a bit of physical exercise, get some colour in his cheeks, but amazingly, it never came. '*Love* that book!' exclaimed Hamish, sounding like he actually meant it. 'Read it when I was a bairn. One of my all time favourites, that is.'

'Really?' Tom was genuinely surprised. Hamish had never struck him as the sort that enjoyed reading anything more challenging than *The Sun*.

'Oh, absolutely. Such characters! Long John Silver, Ben Gunn, Blind Pew . . . I tell you what, every pirate film that's ever been made owes a big thank you to

Robert Louis Stevenson. Never mind Johnny Depp, RLS is the guv'nor.' He thought for a moment. 'You know, there's a Writers' Museum in Edinburgh that's got a whole room about him. Perhaps we could pay it a visit some time. If you'd like to, that is.'

'That would be . . . cool,' muttered Tom.

And it didn't end there. When they got to the house, the place had been transformed, freshly decorated from top to bottom, including Tom's bedroom, which had formerly belonged to Hamish's oldest son. The last time Tom had stayed there it had been decorated with tatty old Hibs posters, flags and plastic trophies. Now it looked cool, clean and completely free of clutter.

'We wanted to make it nice for you,' enthused Mum. 'What do you think?'

Tom looked around, badly wanting to vent some teenage spleen by grunting a monosyllabic reply but instead found himself breaking into a smile.

'It looks great,' he admitted. 'Thanks, Mum.' He turned to look at Hamish who was standing in the doorway, clearly seeking approval. 'And Hamish,' he added. 'Seriously, it looks fantastic.'

Hamish grinned with evident relief and advanced into the room. 'Did it all myself,' he announced. 'Only took a day or so.'

'You haven't heard the best part yet,' said Mum. She looked at Hamish. 'You tell him,' she suggested.

'All right.' Hamish reached into his back pocket and pulled out his wallet. For a moment, Tom thought he was going to be presented with some money, but as it turned out it was even better than that. Hamish reached into the wallet and whipped out three brightly coloured tickets. 'We heard about this Hogmanay concert,' he said. 'Thought it sounded like something you might enjoy. According to your dad, you're a bit of a fan of these guys.'

Tom stared at the tickets in mute disbelief. He'd had no idea that The Deceivers were playing an open-air concert in Princes Street Gardens on New Year's Eve. But apparently they were and here were three tickets to the event. 'Of course,' added Hamish, 'you'll have to drag us old-timers along with you, but if you've no objection to that?'

Tom finally found his voice. 'Wow!' he said. 'Thanks, Hamish, that's . . . that's just the best. Really, thank you.' The two of them stood looking at each other for a moment and it occurred to Tom that Hamish was probably hoping for a hug at this point, so he hastily defused the situation by reaching out and shaking the man's hand, which, based on their previous encounters, was very like genuine progress. He didn't feel quite ready for the hug thing yet.

'You're welcome,' said Hamish. 'My pleasure.'

Hamish continued to behave himself. On Christmas Eve the three of them drove up to Falkirk to meet Hamish's brother and their family and Tom watched in amazement as Hamish steadfastly refused all offers of alcohol, telling everyone that he would be driving home later and needed to keep a clear head. Even Mum said that he could have *one* drink and still drive, but he'd stuck with several glasses of Diet Coke instead. And now here they were, the three of them, driving back to Fairmilehead in Hamish's car, Mum chatting happily away in the passenger seat and Tom in the back, reading *Treasure Island* on the illuminated screen of the Kindle.

He'd just got to a really exciting bit, where Jim Hawkins and his companions had taken refuge in the stockade, when something made him glance up from the book. A strange feeling, a vaguely light-headed sensation that was all too familiar to him . . . the feeling that he knew from experience often affected him shortly before one of his little trips into the past. He looked towards the windscreen and there was a magpie, sitting alone on a crash barrier as the car sped around a long curve in the road. It stayed absolutely still, seemingly unafraid of the sound of the approaching vehicle, staring straight towards it as it drew closer, its tiny black eyes reflecting the beam of the headlights. Then the car was accelerating around the bend and the bird was lost to sight, but Tom felt a powerful sense of foreboding. Wasn't a single magpie supposed to be unlucky? What was the old poem, he remembered from primary school? *One for sorrow, two for joy . . .*

Mum and Hamish didn't seem to have noticed the bird, they were chatting happily away, discussing something that Hamish's elderly grandmother had said back at the party. She'd got confused about the meal they were eating and announced that the fresh salmon they'd been served was the oddest tasting turkey she'd ever had. Mum and Hamish broke out laughing and Tom saw that Hamish had turned his head slightly to look at Mum, that he wasn't watching the road as the car came out of the curve and accelerated into the straight.

That was when Tom saw the figure gliding across the road in front of them, a tall, imposing figure in a long leather cape, the man's face hidden behind a crow-like mask, a mask that even now was turning towards the car to stare as the vehicle bore down on him.

And Tom opened his mouth and yelled, 'Hamish, look out!'

Everything seemed to happen in slow motion after that. He was aware of Hamish wrenching the steering wheel hard to the left and he was also aware of the car tilting to one side, brakes squealing in protest. He heard Mum give a long shrill scream and then they were swaying sickeningly through the air, passing by the masked figure and hurtling headlong towards the crash barrier. There was an impact that Tom felt in his bones but weirdly, didn't *hear* and quite suddenly the windscreen was transformed into a crazed mess that he could no longer see through, although he felt the motion of the journey in his guts as the car arced forward and down. He steeled himself for the impact when it hit the ground.

But when the sensation came it was exactly something he had experienced before, a soft treacly blackness that seemed to spill through him like a dark tide. The pain he'd anticipated didn't happen. As he went down into the dark there was a brief flapping of wings and a lone magpie fluttered briefly past him, but it was the last thing he saw for quite some time.

Two

He came slowly back to his senses, but even as they returned to him, bit-by-bit, he knew that he was back again, that he was no longer in his own time. He knew it with a grim certainty, even before he registered that the gloomy interior he was sprawled in wasn't Hamish's familiar hatchback, but an altogether different kind of vehicle. His nostrils filled with the smell of leather and wood and the musky tang of some kind of animal.

He was lying in a foetal position amidst a litter of smashed glass and the square window immediately beneath him framed nothing more than a pattern of rough cobblestones. He stirred himself and looked upwards, to see another smashed window revealing a view of the night sky, sprinkled with a generous helping of stars. When he looked to his right, where he might have expected to see Mum and Hamish, he saw only another leather seat rising vertically in front of him and behind it, nothing but a smooth board covered in maroon velvet. His brain began to make sense of his surroundings and he realised that whatever vehicle he was in, it was lying on its side. With some considerable effort he managed to get to his feet, standing on the cobbles. He braced himself and reaching upwards, he grabbed the window frame above him and pulled himself through it. It was only on emerging that he realised he'd just been inside an old fashioned four-wheeled carriage that had overturned. He crouched for a moment, looking around. The narrow street seemed deserted, the tall buildings looming over the stricken vehicle, but oddly, the accident seemed to have attracted no attention. Ahead of him, also lying on its side was a horse, still harnessed to the coach, though there was no sign of a driver.

'What now?' muttered Tom.

He dropped over the side of the coach onto solid ground and walked around to examine the horse. Its chest was rising and falling, its eyes staring wildly at nothing in particular. As Tom watched, it made an attempt to struggle upright, but the harness held it in position and it snorted, fell back again, shook its head.

'Whoah, boy.' Tom patted the creature's flank in an attempt to calm it, but this seemed to have the opposite effect and the horse tried once again to get itself upright. Worried that it might hurt itself, Tom crouched beside the horse and began to free it from its harness, a skill he'd picked up when working at Laird's Lodging House in 1824. After a few minutes of frantic tugging and unbuckling, he had the restraints undone and the horse finally managed to struggle to its feet. Then, without so much as pausing for breath, it trotted briskly away along the road, its head turning this way and that as if searching for the direction that would take it home. After a few moments it disappeared around a corner, but Tom could still hear the hollow clopping of hooves on unseen cobbles for quite some time.

He stared down the street for a moment and then turned back to look at the coach. One wheel was still turning, so it was clear that it hadn't been lying here for long. The accident must only just have happened, but if that was the case, where was everybody? He opened his mouth to shout for help and in that instant, a church bell, somewhere nearby, tolled the hour. Three a.m.! No wonder the streets were deserted. Tom stood, looking around, trying to identify his surroundings. He was in Edinburgh, he was sure of that, but it wasn't a street he recognised from earlier visits and for the moment at least, he had no idea in which direction he should go.

He began to remember what had happened in Hamish's car, just before everything had gone haywire; the familiar cloaked figure that had drifted across the road. He glanced nervously around, paying particular reference to the many narrow alleyways dotting each side of the street. For the moment at least, he appeared to be completely alone.

He told himself that he couldn't stand there all night, and besides, what if he got blamed for the accident? No, he'd just have to do what he always did at such times and seek refuge. Only now, as the adrenalin began to subside, did he register that it was bitterly cold. Whatever year he had stumbled in to, it still felt like late December. He shrugged his coat tighter around him and began to walk, looking for something he recognised.

As he walked, he slipped a hand into his pocket, expecting to find his mobile phone there. But then he remembered he'd forgotten to take it to the party with him, that he'd left it on the bedside cabinet in his room at Hamish's house. This was a blow. On his previous journeys into the past, he'd had a phone with him, a touch of 21st century technology that he could use to prove to the people he met that he was from another time. All he had with him on this trip was a handful of assorted coins. He cursed his forgetfulness.

He neared the top of the street and looked left and right along an intersecting road, trying to get his bearings. To his left, he saw the familiar silhouette of Edinburgh Castle, looking strangely menacing under the light of a full moon. Instinct made him turn towards it and walk slightly downhill, his eyes swinging left and right to seek out possible areas of ambush.

He came to a narrow alleyway on his left and hesitated as he heard the sound of a low moan, issuing from out of the shadows. His first instinct was to run, but when he looked into the alleyway he saw the figure of a man lying on his back, looking imploringly up at him. Tom hesitated, suspecting that the stranger might be trying to lure him into the alley where others could be lying in wait, but the man's thin, pale features suggested that he really was in trouble and a shaft of moonlight filtering into the alley revealed that blood was dribbling down his chin.

'Please . . .' he croaked. 'Help me.'

Tom edged closer. He could see now that the stranger was in his late twenties or early thirties, his gaunt but striking features framed by long dark hair. He had a thick, carefully shaped moustache and there was the hint of a tiny v-shaped beard under his bottom lip. It was the oddest thing, but something about the man seemed familiar to Tom, as though he'd met him somewhere recently, although he couldn't think where.

Against his better judgement he stepped into the alleyway and stood for a moment looking down at the man. 'Are you all right?' he asked and immediately felt stupid, because he so clearly wasn't. 'Are you sick?'

The man gave a ragged cough. 'I was . . . heading home after a night's carousing with some . . . good friends and I . . . missed my footing in the dark. I feel ridiculous.' He had a refined Edinburgh accent and seemed to be having difficulty in drawing breath. 'I have a . . . condition of the lungs, you see. It is my scourge, I'm afraid. I wonder, young sir . . . if you might be so kind as to help me to stand up again?'

Tom decided there was nothing for it. He could hardly clear off and leave the man lying here in the freezing cold. He crouched and allowed the stranger to slip an arm around his shoulders, registering as he did so his shockingly thin frame. With some difficulty Tom managed to straighten up, lifting the man back to his feet. In doing so, Tom couldn't help noticing the powerful smell of whisky on his breath.

'How long have you been lying here?' he inquired.

'Not sure. I . . . I blacked out for a while. What time is it?'

'Just after three, I think.'

'Quite some time, then. It was around midnight when I left my companions.' He groaned and lifted his free hand to his forehead.

Tom frowned. 'Are you, are you drunk?' he asked.

'Good heavens, no! Slightly under the influence, but . . . not excessively so. And after all, it is . . . almost Christmas.' He looked at Tom and gave a weak smile. 'So, to whom do I have the pleasure?'

'Sorry?'

'Your name, son, so I can . . . thank my saviour.'

'Oh, I'm Tom. Tom Afflick.'

'And I'm Lou. At least that's what my friends call me. A pleasure to make your acquaintance.' He took a deep breath and seemed to try and steady himself. 'I wonder, Tom, if I might . . . impose upon your good nature a trifle longer?'

'Er . . . well I'm not sure, I . . .'

'I need a guide.'

'I'm a bit lost myself, to tell you the truth.'

'Oh, I know my way well enough. I just can't . . . quite make it under my own steam.' Lou gave a dry chuckle, which turned into another hacking cough. Flecks of blood spattered his chin and he reached into a coat pocket and withdrew a white handkerchief. He mopped at his lips and Tom noticed that the linen was already liberally flecked with spots of red. 'I wonder, would you please be so kind as to help me home? It's not very far and I promise you'll be rewarded for your efforts.'

Tom considered his options. It wasn't as if he had any other plans. 'All right,' he said. 'Which way?'

Lou indicated that they should leave the alley and continue onwards so that was what they did, Lou leaning heavily on Tom's shoulders. As they limped slowly along the street, Lou attempted to make conversation.

'That accent of yours,' he said. 'I'd wager you're English, but . . . not a Londoner.'

'No, I'm from Manchester.'

'Ah. That isn't a city I know well. What brings you to *Auld Reekie*?'

'Umm . . .' A good question, decided Tom, but not one that could easily be answered. He decided to stretch the truth a little. 'My mother lives here. I'm just up for Christmas.'

'You're out late.'

'Yes, well like you, I was . . . visiting some friends.'

They reached another intersection and Lou waved a hand to his right. They swayed around the corner.

'I'm sort of visiting myself,' said Lou. 'I was . . . in Davos until recently.'

Tom frowned. 'Davos?' he muttered. He thought it sounded like a character from *Doctor Who*.

'In Switzerland. We usually winter there. The doctors assure me it's . . . better for my . . . health.' He laughed bitterly but it quickly turned into another cough, obliging him to wipe his mouth again. 'But, I . . . couldn't resist the lure of Hogmanay in . . . my home city. No doubt my dear wife will use this as an excuse to send us straight back to the Alpine air. She's a . . . remarkable woman, but . . . something of a worrier.' He looked at Tom. 'How old are you?' he inquired.

'I'm fourteen.'

Lou nodded. 'Just a year older than Lloyd,' he said. 'My stepson.' He hesitated for a moment. 'Look, do you mind if we stand for a bit?' he whispered. 'I need to . . . get my . . . breath back.'

'No, of course not.' Tom took the opportunity to study the long stretch of street ahead of him, identifying as he did so, a dozen places where somebody might be lying in wait. He wondered what would happen if McSweeny suddenly jumped out at them. Would he just leave Lou to his fate and get out of there? Or try to defend him? But then, he reasoned, McSweeny wasn't after Lou, was he?

After a few moments Lou's breathing seemed to settle and he indicated that they should be on their way again. 'It's not so very far now,' he told Tom. 'Fran will probably have the entire Edinburgh constabulary out looking for me.' He glanced at Tom. 'How far away are you from home?'

Another good question. 'A long way,' said Tom and hoped that Lou wouldn't enquire further.

'Well, since I've . . . taken you off your route . . . I'm sure we might find you a berth for the night. Seems the least we can do. That way you can meet Lloyd in the morning.' Lou pointed along the street and indicated a row of imposing Victorian houses at the far end. 'That's where we're headed,' he said. 'We're renting a house down there for a few days.'

Tom nodded. 'Can I ask you a question?'

'Certainly.'

'It's going to sound a bit odd.'

'That's all right. I'm rather fond of odd questions.'

'Good. All right, then.' Tom took a deep breath. 'Erm . . . what I really want to know is, what year is it?'

Three

Lou stopped in his tracks and Tom was obliged to wait for a moment.

'You don't know what year it is?' muttered Lou.

'Er . . . no, I've . . . kind of forgotten.'

'I see.' Lou lifted a hand to pull at his moustache. 'You're right,' he admitted. 'That *does* seem strange.' He shrugged, carried on walking again. 'Well, since you ask, it's eighteen eighty-one,' he said.

Tom did some quick mental calculations. Fifty-six years later than his last visit. But what, he wondered, had drawn him to this particular year? He knew from previous experience that there tended to be an anchor, something that drew him to a particular time and place. At Mary King's Close, it had been Morag's ghost that had reeled him in. In the National Museum of Scotland, the tiny coffins, displayed in a glass case had taken him to 1828, the year they'd been created. But Hamish's car on a lonely stretch of Edinburgh road? Surely there was nothing there to connect him with 1881?

'A penny for them,' said Lou and Tom looked at him.

'I beg your pardon?'

'A penny for your thoughts.' He smiled. 'It looked like you have . . . a lot on your mind.'

'You've no idea,' Tom assured him.

They were nearing the long curving terrace of townhouses now. In one of them every window seemed to be glowing with yellow light. Lou sighed. 'What did I tell you?' he muttered. 'All lit up like Jenners department store. Fran will have assumed I'm lying dead in a ditch somewhere.' He indicated a short flight of steep, stone steps up to the door and Tom helped him up them, Lou using his free hand to support himself on the cast iron railings that edged the steps. They got to the top and Lou reached out and pulled the bell cord. A shrill clanging seemed to echo throughout the house. 'Now we're for it,' muttered Lou and he winked at Tom.

They didn't have to wait for very long. The door swung open and a formidable-looking woman stood there, glaring out at the newcomers. She was considerably older than Lou, Tom decided, her black hair tied up in a bun. She had piercing dark eyes and a prominent chin. She looked, Tom thought, extremely cross.

'Lou, where in the name of heaven have you been? I've been going out of my mind with worry!' She had an American accent, Tom decided, and a very domineering manner. It sounded like she was talking to a little boy.

'Now, Fran, there's no need to make a fuss . . . I just . . .'

'There's *every* need! Why I allowed you to talk me into coming back to this godforsaken city is beyond me. And why did I let you out with those reprobate friends of yours? I ought to have my head tested.' She noticed the smear of dried blood on Lou's chin and stepped closer. 'Lou, you're bleeding again!'

'It's nothing, dear, just the usual problem. I'll be right as rain, once I've rested.' Lou indicated Tom. 'This young gentleman was . . . kind enough to help me back,' he explained. 'He tells me he's far from home himself, so I thought . . . we might offer him a bed for the night?'

Frances gazed at Tom for a moment, and frowned as though she wasn't particularly keen on the idea. But then she seemed to soften and beckoned the two of them inside.

'Well, don't stand there on the cold step all night, come in, COME IN!'

Tom did as he was told, helping Lou into the hallway and along it to a large sitting room. Lou indicated an armchair in front of a slumbering fire and Tom steered him towards it. Lou removed his overcoat, handed it to his wife and slumped down with a sign of relief. 'I suppose Lloyd is asleep?' he asked.

'Yes, of *course* he is, as we all should be. It's half past three in the morning! One of these days you're going to heed the advice of the doctors and start having early nights. And I don't suppose I even need to ask if you've been drinking whisky?'

Frances seemed to remember there was somebody else there and she smiled apologetically at Tom. 'Thank you so much for bringing him home,' she said. She held out a hand. 'Shall I take your coat?'

Tom slipped off the overcoat he was wearing and handed it to her then realised that Lou and Frances were staring at him in alarm. He was quite used to this effect. At that moment he was wearing blue jeans, purple trainers and a brightly-coloured t-shirt featuring an image of a gorilla wearing a suit and a top hat. A caption in bright orange letters read **GO APE!**

'Is that what passes for fashion in Manchester?' asked Lou.

'You'll get used to it,' Tom assured him. He took a seat on a sofa opposite Lou. 'It's just, well, we dress a bit differently to other cities.'

Lou pointed to the image on the t-shirt. 'What's the significance of that?' he asked.

'Oh, er, it's just saying, you know, go a bit wild? Let out your dark side?' He looked from Lou to Frances and back again. 'Everyone's wearing them in Manchester.'

Frances was the first to recover. 'Yes, well I know it's late, but I dare say a cup of something hot wouldn't go amiss?'

'I could murder a latte,' said Tom, and then, noting the look of bafflement on Frances's face, added. 'Er, whatever you've got.'

'I was thinking of cocoa,' she said.

'Couldn't Anna get that?' suggested Lou.

'I sent her to bed ages ago,' Frances told him. 'You

can't expect hired staff to stay up till all hours just because you take it into your head to go out carousing. But don't worry, I'm quite capable of making a cup of cocoa.' She hurried away, taking the coats with her. Tom and Lou were left smiling at each other in companionable silence. Lou picked up a poker from beside the fire and stirred the slumbering coals, then threw on a few more chunks from a brass scuttle beside it. Tom looked around the room. It was a nice enough place and there was a small Christmas tree in one corner of the room, adorned with baubles, but otherwise the room seemed devoid of the kind of knick-knacks you'd expect to find in a real home. He remembered that Lou had said that he was only staying here for a few days.

Lou seemed to read Tom's thoughts and said, 'It's not much of a tree, this year. The best we could scrounge up at short notice. Normally, of course, we'd have stayed with my parents at Heriot Row, but I rather fancied some time in my home city away from them. They don't even know we're here!' He looked for a moment like a mischievous boy, confessing to some prank. His breathing seemed to have settled a little now that he was sitting down. 'So I'm afraid we could only bring a few bits and pieces with us. Some of Lloyd's toys, naturally, he'd never have forgiven us if we'd brought him nothing to play with. And one or two of my books. I'm afraid I have an awful lot of them.'

'Oh, you're a keen reader then?'

'You could say that.'

Tom noticed a magazine lying on the arm of the sofa and picking it up, he glanced at the cover. The title of the magazine was *Young Folks*, so he assumed that this must be one of Lloyd's things.

'Ah, that's the latest edition,' said Lou, rather puzzlingly. 'If you have time to look at it while you're here, I'd be glad of your opinion.'

'My opinion?' Tom leafed idly through it, not quite understanding the comment. He paused at a pen and ink illustration of what looked like a pirate standing on the deck of a sailing ship, a fierce-looking fellow dressed in a tricorn hat. He had a wooden leg and a parrot was sitting on one of his shoulders.

'This guy looks like Long John Silver,' observed Tom.

'He *is*,' said Lou and he gave Tom a strange look. 'So . . . you're familiar with the story? You must already be a reader of *Young Folks*.'

'This?' Tom shook his head. 'No, I've never heard of it.'

Lou scowled. 'Then . . . I don't really understand. How do you know the name?' he demanded.

'What name?'

'Long John Silver.'

'Well, because *everyone* knows . . .' Tom hesitated, as a thought occurred to him. He looked again at the page and this time, registered the title of the story. *Treasure Island, or, the Mutiny of the Hispaniola*. And then the name of the author: Captain George North. He returned his gaze to Lou. 'But, this is, it's the same story as—' he looked again at the title. 'Who's Captain George North?' he demanded.

Lou smiled. 'I am,' he said, with a grin. 'It's a pen name.'

'But that means . . .' Realisation struck Tom like a sledgehammer blow to the skull. 'Oh my God,' he said. 'You're Robert Louis Stevenson.'

Just then the door swung open and Frances came into the room, bearing a tray heaped with cups, saucers and a silver jug. 'Now,' she said brightly. 'Who'd like a cup of cocoa?'

Four

They sat drinking their cocoa in a strained silence. Lou was staring at Tom, as if trying to fathom something out, and Tom was piecing recent events together, remembering how he'd been reading *Treasure Island* just before Hamish's car had gone off the road. So *that* was the anchor that had brought him here! He also realised exactly why Lou had seemed so familiar when he'd first seen him. The first page of the Kindle book had featured an old photograph of the author. If only he'd managed to bring the Kindle back with him . . . although, if he *had* done that, how would he ever explain its existence to Lou?

Eventually, Lou could hold his peace no longer. 'Forgive me, Tom, but I don't really understand how you know who I am.'

'Well, I . . . I've read your stuff, obviously,' said Tom.

Lou and Frances exchanged puzzled looks. 'What stuff?' asked Lou. 'I've hardly published anything.' He thought for a moment. '*Edinburgh: Picturesque*

Notes? Nobody's read that. *Latter-Day Arabian Nights?* I doubt it. And I don't think for one moment that you've read *Virginibus Puerisque*?'

'Virgy-what?' muttered Tom.

'I rest my case. So it *must* have been that story.' He pointed to the magazine, which now lay draped over the arm of the sofa. 'It's the only thing I've done that would be suitable for somebody of your age. But you claim you've never heard of *Young Folks*, so . . .'

'Well, I . . . I suppose I've read another version of it,' said Tom, evasively. 'Yeah, that'll be it. The one with your real name on it.'

'No such version exists,' cried Lou.

'There *was* some talk of publishing it as a novel,' Frances reminded him.

'Aye and that's all it ever will be,' Lou assured her. 'Talk.'

'But didn't Mr Henderson say something about showing it to contacts he has in the book publishing trade?'

'Henderson talks a good game. But the twelve shillings and sixpence he pays me per column is all the revenue we're ever likely to see from *that* story. And from what he said in his last letter, it's hardly set the world of children's literature alight. If anything, sales are *down*.'

'Yes, but perhaps a book . . .'

'Fran, you're very kind, But I hardly think something that was created to keep Lloyd occupied on a rainy day is ever going to be published beyond the covers of a weekly magazine.'

'Oh, it could be,' Tom assured him. 'Just give it time.' He picked up the magazine and turned back to the relevant page. He did an exaggerated double-take. 'Oh wait a minute,' he said. 'Yes, *Young Folks*! Yes, I *did* read it here. But I . . . forgot. Probably because of that title . . .'

Lou gave him a sharp look. 'What's wrong with it?'

'Hmm? Oh well, it's a bit long-winded, isn't it?'

Lou waved a hand in exasperation. 'Oh, you can blame James Henderson for that. The editor of the magazine. He didn't like my original title, so he took it upon himself to change it after a few episodes. What I had was much simpler. *The Sea Cook*.'

'The *what*?'

'*The Sea Cook: A Story for Boys*. Much better, don't you think?'

Tom frowned. 'I'm not being funny, but I can see why he changed it.'

'Oh, indeed? And why's that?'

'Well, it's a bit dull, isn't it? You may as well have called it *The Wool Glove*.'

Lou looked offended. 'Oh, forgive me. I didn't realise I was in the presence of a literary expert!'

'I'm not an expert,' Tom assured him. 'I just think it could do with something a bit . . . edgier, you know. A bit more memorable.'

'Such as?'

Tom took a deep breath, realising as he did so, that he was about to do something incredibly momentous. 'Well, it's kind of there already,' he said, pointing to the title. 'Only it's lost in the rest of it.'

'What is?' Lou looked baffled.

Tom pointed. 'I was thinking . . . you should just call it *Treasure Island*?'

Lou scowled. 'That's a wee bit simplistic for a title, don't you think?'

'No, I think it works, big time! Easy to remember. And it's got a nice ring to it. Trust me, that's what you should call it.'

'But . . . Long John Silver is the main character in the story and he *is* a sea cook, so . . .'

'Jim Hawkins is the main character,' Tom corrected him. 'And you didn't call it *The Kid That Worked in The Admiral Benbow*, did you?'

'Of course not! That would be a ridiculous title.'

'There you go then. Mind you, you've got lots of great characters in here. Ben Gunn, Blind Pew, Israel Hands . . .' He remembered something that Hamish had told him. 'Every pirate film that's ever been made owes a big thank you to this story.'

'Every pirate *what*?' muttered Lou.

'Er, every . . . umm . . . pirate *thing*,' stammered Tom. He realised he was rapidly getting into hot water, so he changed the subject. 'You were saying you wrote the book for your stepson?'

'It's not a book,' insisted Lou. 'It's a weekly adventure in a magazine. There's a big difference.'

'Yes, but perhaps Tom has a point,' argued Frances. 'About the title, I mean. I never really liked *The Sea Cook*.'

'That's news to me, Fran.'

'Oh, Lou, you know perfectly well! I said from the

very beginning, I thought it gave a reader no idea about the adventure in the story.' She looked suddenly rather excited. 'You remember how you read it out to us every night at Miss McGregor's cottage in Braemar? I was every bit as captivated as Lloyd was. Who knows? Maybe it really *does* deserve a wider audience than just the readers of *Young Folks*.'

'I seem to remember people being rather excited when I got the offer,' said Lou, a little irritably. 'Suddenly, young Tom here arrives and everybody's talking about a book. I mean, let's not get ahead of ourselves. It's just a wee throwaway story.'

'Oh no, it's better than that,' said Tom. 'What you've got here . . .' He patted the magazine, 'is something that's going to last forever.'

Lou scoffed. 'As long as it lasts until we need some more kindling for the fire,' he said, 'I'm happy.'

Frances looked outraged. 'Now you know that's stuff and nonsense,' she told him. 'I have a pristine copy of every issue stored safely away and that one will be joining the others just as soon as Lloyd's finished reading it.'

'Hmph.' Lou seemed to slump into a mood. 'Everybody seems to think they know better than I do,' he observed. 'Don't mind me, I'm just the author of the damned thing.'

'Oh, stop being such a grump!' exclaimed Frances. 'Let's drink up our cocoa and get to bed before the dawn breaks.' She looked at Tom. 'I've put you in the guest room,' she told him. 'I've already lit the gas light in there. It isn't much but there's a decent bed, so you should be comfortable enough.'

'Thanks,' said Tom. 'I'll be fine.' He looked at Lou. 'I just want to say it *is* a fantastic story. I read half of it on the train here from Manchester.'

'You must be a very slow reader,' observed Lou cuttingly.

'Oh, I took the fast train,' Tom assured him.

Lou studied him for a few moments. 'There's something altogether mysterious about you,' he said. 'I don't know exactly what it is, but . . . you seem to know more than you should about an awful lot of things.' He pointed at Tom's t-shirt. 'And who dresses like that? Nobody I've ever met.'

'Now, Lou, you'll make our guest feel uncomfortable,' Frances chided him. She set down her empty cup and got up from the sofa. 'Come along, Tom, I'll show you where you'll be sleeping.'

Tom got to his feet. 'Thanks. Goodnight, Lou,' he said.

'And goodnight to you, Tom. Maybe the two of us can have a wee talk in the morning.'

Tom followed Frances out of the room and up a flight of stairs. She opened a door on the first landing to reveal a large, bare room with a single bed and a few pieces of furniture. A single gas lamp on the wall filled the room with a soft glow.

'If I'd known you were coming, I'd have got Anna to tidy up in here,' she told him. 'And to light a fire.' She pointed to the lamp. 'You can turn it off when you're ready to go to sleep.' She smiled at him. 'Thank you again for looking after Lou. His state of health is such a constant worry. I was going out of my mind when he didn't come home on time.'

'Oh, no problem,' Tom assured her. 'I just . . . happened to be there.' He frowned. 'What exactly is wrong with him?' he asked.

'It's tuberculosis,' said Frances. 'It's always worse in cold weather. That's why I was so set against the idea of coming back here for Christmas, but Lou is stubborn. When he gets a notion in his head there's no dissuading him. And he wouldn't even tell his parents we were coming here. I know they don't really approve of me, but . . .'

'Why not?' asked Tom.

'Oh, you know, the divorced woman and all that. People in this part of the world can be terribly stuffy.' She thought for a moment. 'I haven't even asked about your circumstances,' she said. 'Lou said something about you being far from home?'

'Yeah,' said Tom. 'Yeah, I am. But that's ok, I'm kind of used to it.'

She seemed about to say something else, but seemed to think better of it. 'Well, in that case, we'll see you in the morning,' she said. 'I hope you sleep well.' She went out of the room, closing the door behind her. Tom stood for a moment, looking around. Then he walked across to the window and pulled back the curtain to peek outside. Below him was the cobbled street, illuminated by a row of gas lamps. It was silent out there and he was glad to note that there was no sign of a cloaked figure prowling in the shadows. He had hoped that he was finally rid of William McSweeny, but he couldn't forget that glimpse of him gliding across the road in front of Hamish's car. Chances were he would appear again and if he did, Tom needed to be ready for him. But for the moment at least, he felt exhausted.

He let the curtain fall back, walked over to the bed and sat down. He unlaced his shoes but it was cold in the room, so he didn't take off anything else. Experience had taught him that there was no sense in fretting about his situation. All he could do was go with the flow and hope that eventually, something would happen to take him back to his own time. In the meantime he was the guest of one of the world's greatest authors, even if that author had no idea of the kind of fame that awaited him. It was a situation that a million historians would have given their life savings to replicate.

Tom crawled under the covers and closed his eyes. He was tired and ready for sleep, but just as he drifted away, he was vaguely aware of a brief fluttering of black and white feathers, somewhere in the air above his head.

Five

Sunlight spilled onto Tom's face and he opened his eyes, blinked a couple of times and then sat up with a gasp as he realised that somebody was standing right beside the bed, staring intently down at him. His eyes came into focus and he saw, to his relief, that it was just a thin boy around his own age. The boy had short, dark hair, a sullen expression and the same piercing eyes as his mother. He was dressed in a sort of pale blue velvet sailor suit with an elaborate white lace collar. He looked, even making allowances for the fashions of the period, a real dork in that getup.

'You must be Lloyd,' said Tom.

'And you must be the stranger that's got Lou in such a tizz,' said Lloyd. Like his mother, he had a strong American accent.

'That would be me,' admitted Tom. He yawned, pushed the covers aside and swung his legs over the edge of the bed. Lloyd stared at him in apparent amazement. Then he laughed. 'You dress peculiar.'

'Look who's talking,' muttered Tom. He located his trainers and Lloyd watched as he laced them up.

'I've never seen shoes like those before,' he said. 'What colour do you call that?' Before Tom could answer, the boy prodded him in the chest. 'And what's that supposed to be?' He was referring, Tom supposed, to the image of the gorilla wearing a suit.

'It's just a picture,' muttered Tom. 'It doesn't really mean anything.'

'But how did it get on your clothing? Did somebody paint it on?'

Tom decided this was way too complicated to get into. He finished lacing his shoes and got to his feet. 'Is there a loo around here?' he asked.

'A what?' Lloyd looked mystified.

'I mean, a . . . toilet?' No reaction. 'A . . . lavatory?'

'Oh sure, follow me.' Lloyd led him out of the room and along the landing. Tom noticed now that, despite criticising Tom's trainers, the kid was wearing shiny black shoes with silver buckles on them. He paused in front of another doorway. 'There you go.'

'Thanks.' Tom went into the room and closed the door after him. He was pleased to see a flushing water closet, a luxury he hadn't been granted on his previous visits, but he was rather less happy to note that there was nowhere to wash his hands. He emptied his bladder and zipped himself up. When he came out of the toilet, Lloyd was still standing there, waiting for him. 'Mama says you want Lou to change his title,' he said.

'Er, I *did* kind of suggest it,' admitted Tom.

'I don't see that it's got anything to do with you,' said Lloyd. 'That's *our* story. Lou and I worked on it together.'

'Really?' Tom was unconvinced. 'You *wrote* some of it?'

'Well, no, I didn't actually *write* it, but I saw the map he drew and I asked him to make up a story about it. And if I hadn't done that, I guess there wouldn't *be* a story. So it's kind of half-mine, anyway, right?'

Tom shrugged. 'Maybe. Anyway, I only suggested another title. It's no big deal. Don't you think that long one sounds a bit . . . meh?'

'A bit what?'

'You know. Dull. I mean, it was just an idea, he doesn't have to . . .'

'Mama says that Lou is all fired up over it. Says he didn't get a wink of sleep last night, thanks to you.'

'Oh, well now, I didn't mean to . . .'

'I think it's a downright liberty, coming here and making suggestions. There's nothing wrong with the title, it's a perfectly good one.'

'That's a matter of opinion,' said Tom. He looked around. 'Where is everybody?' he asked.

'Mama's down in the kitchen. She sent me up to get you. Lou is still in bed, asleep, because *you* got him all fired up so he couldn't rest.'

'Sorry about that.' Tom tried to step around Lloyd, but he moved to bar Tom's path.

'I think from now on you should keep your opinions to yourself.'

Tom glared irritably at Lloyd. The boy was several inches shorter than him and rather puny-looking. It occurred to him it would be fairly easy to just push him out of the way, but he didn't think that would be a good idea, not when he was a guest in somebody's home.

'Excuse me,' he said, and tried to step the other way, but once again Lloyd blocked his path.

'In fact,' he added, 'I think it would be a good thing if you went on your way as soon as possible. Because you're not wanted here.'

Tom almost laughed at that. 'I think that would be up to your mum and dad, wouldn't it?'

'My *what*?'

'Your parents.'

There was a brief silence while they stood there, staring challengingly at each other. 'My father was a Civil War hero,' said Lloyd, mystifyingly. 'He always told me to speak out for myself.'

'Are you an only child?' asked Tom. He wasn't sure why he'd asked the question.

'No, I have an older sister, Belle. She's married and all. But she decided not to spend Christmas with us.'

'I wonder why,' murmured Tom.

'Oh, Lloyd?' Frances's voice called from below. 'Is everything all right, dear? Did you manage to wake Tom?'

'Just coming, Mama!' shouted Lloyd. But he didn't take his eyes off Tom for a moment. He lowered his voice. 'I'm warning you,' he said. 'Keep your nose out of things that don't concern you.' Then he turned and strutted along the landing to the staircase. He paused for a moment and stared back at Tom. 'Well?' he demanded. 'Are you coming or not?'

This time, Tom did laugh. He couldn't help himself.

It was the way Lloyd was trying to act so tough, when he was dressed like *that*. The effect was really comical. Tom followed Lloyd down the stairs and around to the back of the house where there was a large kitchen. A young woman in a white pinafore and matching frilly hat was standing at a cast-iron range, cooking sausages and bacon. Tom assumed this must be Anna, the hired help that Lou had mentioned the night before. Frances was sitting at a large pine table, daintily sipping a cup of tea. She was immaculately dressed as though for some special occasion. Lloyd went straight to the seat beside her and sat down with his arms crossed, as though he was defying Tom to tell him to move, but Frances looked up at Tom and gave him a welcoming smile. 'Ah, good morning,' she said. 'I trust you slept well?'

'Yes, thank you, Mrs Stevenson.'

'Oh, now we'll have none of that! Call me Fran.'

Remembering he needed to wash his hands, Tom went around the table to a sink and operated a pump, splashing cold water onto his hands. Frances looked on in bemusement. 'Is that a Manchester custom?' she asked. 'Washing your hands before breakfast.'

'Pretty much,' said Tom. 'Everyone does it where I come from.' He dried his hands on a towel that was hanging by the sink, then took a seat beside Frances, keeping himself on the far side of the table from Lloyd, who sat there staring at him with open contempt.

'So you two boys have introduced yourselves?' ventured Frances.

'Yes,' said Tom, smiling mockingly at Lloyd. 'We've . . . talked.'

'I imagine the two of you must have plenty in common. Both of you keen readers and all.'

'Yes, Lloyd was just telling me how he helped Lou write *Treasure Island*,' said Tom.

'Indeed? A little exaggeration there, I think.' She shot Lloyd a reproving look. 'But it was very strange how it transpired. We took a cottage in Braemar for the summer, out in the wilds. We pictured ourselves enjoying picnics in the sunshine but the weather was just awful. I think it must have poured with rain every day we were there. So we were left to amuse ourselves indoors, as best we could. And one day, Lloyd and Lou drew this little map on a sheet of paper . . .'

'See,' said Lloyd. 'What did I tell you?'

Frances ignored him. 'Then Lou started writing in the names of all these made-up places. Finally, he wrote the words, *Treasure Island* on the paper and explained that this was a place where pirates buried their booty. And Lloyd begged Lou to tell him a story about the island and of course, that's how it all began. Lou went into one of his wild passions about the idea and he wrote all day, every day. Looking back, it's a good job the weather *was* bad, for we saw hardly anything of him in the daytime. He would read us a chapter each night, sitting by the fire and . . . well, almost before we knew it, he had fifteen chapters and that's when it all began to get more serious.'

'So, he'd already come up with the best title,' observed Tom. 'But then he changed it.'

'It's called *The Wreck of the Hispaniola*,' insisted Lloyd.

'Yes, dear, we know what it's called,' said Frances, calmly. 'But it's true that the first thing he wrote down was . . .'

'*He* wants Papa to change it,' snarled Lloyd, pointing at Tom, as though he thought his mother might have missed this point.

'*He* has a name,' said Frances, frostily. 'And it would be more polite if you'd use it.'

Lloyd grunted, but continued to stare challengingly at Tom. 'I don't think it's any of his business, coming here and telling Papa to change the title of his story,' he said. 'Who is he anyway? Just some stranger who turned up in the middle of the night and started . . .'

'Lloyd Samuel Stevenson, we'll have none of that attitude at the breakfast table,' said Frances, forcefully and Lloyd was obliged to stop talking. He hung his head and looked glumly at his hands. 'Tom is our guest here and we always treat our guests with the greatest respect.'

'That's absolutely right,' said a voice and glancing up, Tom saw that Lou had just entered the kitchen. He was dressed in a velvet jacket and his hair was tousled as though he'd just got out of bed.

'Lou, you should have slept longer,' Frances chided him. 'You barely had a wink of sleep all night.'

'The smell of frying bacon roused me,' he told her and he took a seat beside Lloyd. He ruffled the boy's hair affectionately and then smiled across the table at Tom. 'You got me thinking last night,' he said.

'Did I?'

'Yes.' Lou leaned closer, looking Tom directly

in the eye. 'Maybe my little story *does* deserve a wider audience.'

At this Tom couldn't help noticing the expression on Lloyd's face – as though somebody had just kicked him, very hard in the stomach.

'And I'm thinking that perhaps it could revert to the original title of *The Sea Cook: A Story for Boys*.'

'Maybe not that bit,' muttered Tom, but Lou ignored him.

'So with this in mind, I have just written to Long John Silver himself, to suggest . . . nay, *demand*, that he introduce me to some more of his contacts in the world of publishing.'

Tom was puzzled by the last remark and his expression must have shown this because Frances leaned closer and said, 'Our friend, Mr William Henley. A writer too, of poetry mostly. He was very much an inspiration for Long John Silver. He is a one-legged gentleman, you see.'

'Oh, right,' said Tom. 'I didn't know that.'

'No reason why you should,' said Frances.

'I've written to Dr Jap too,' Lou told her. 'I'm on a crusade here and I intend to leave no stone unturned!'

'It was our friend, Dr Jap, who first introduced Lou to Mr Henderson, the editor of *Young Folks*,' explained Frances.

'Oh, right,' said Tom.

Lloyd looked as though he was now on the verge of tears. 'But Papa, I like *The Wreck of the Hispaniola*!' he complained.

'Well, Lloyd, that's very loyal of you. But we need

to rise above such considerations and think of what's best for the story. Tom here has inspired me to think that perhaps I could do more with my little creation.'

Just then Anna began to ferry over plates of food. Tom was delighted to see that of all the time periods he'd visited, this one seemed to have the best grub. Gone were the foul slops of Mary King's Close in 1645, the rotting throwaways scavenged every morning by Jamie Wilson in 1824 and brought to Laird's Lodging House. In front of him he was delighted to see a full cooked breakfast. Sausages, bacon, fried eggs and as much toast as he could eat.

'Please, don't stand on ceremony,' said Frances. 'As we like to say in San Francisco, dig in!'

Tom needed no second bidding. He began to eat, quickly and greedily, devouring the plate of food in a very short time. Glancing up, he noticed that Lou was barely touching his meal while Lloyd was simply pushing the various items around his plate, an expression of discontent on his face.

'Lloyd, Anna worked very hard on that breakfast, at least try to do it some justice,' said Frances. 'And try to do something about that miserable expression too.' She looked at her husband. 'Surely you must have more appetite than that?'

Lou shrugged his shoulders. 'You know me, my dear. When I have one of my obsessions upon me, I can't think of eating.' Lou studied Tom. 'But surely it's time we heard a little more about our esteemed guest,' he suggested. 'Tom, tell us all about yourself.'

Tom nearly choked on a mouthful of sausage and

had to take a large gulp of tea in order to get it down. 'Oh, there's . . . not much to say,' he spluttered.

'Of course there is. You say you're from Manchester but your mother lives in Edinburgh, right?'

'Er, yes, in Fairmilehead. With my stepfather.'

'Oh?' Lou elbowed Lloyd. 'Sounds like you two have something in common,' he observed and Lloyd's scowl grew darker. 'I know the area, Tom. Lovely, rural setting. In fact, my parents used to rent Swanston Cottage every summer. I have some happy memories of it. I wrote about it in *Picturesque Notes*.'

'Oh, did you?' Tom tried not to panic. 'Well, m . . . my parents live on the . . . the estate.'

'Ah, the farm, you mean! Oh, there's some beautiful thatched cottages there. So, we must have been neighbours. How strange that we never bumped into you as a little boy.'

'Er, yeah. Weird.'

'So, what do your parents do?'

'Oh, erm . . . well, Mum's kind of between jobs.'

'Your mother works?' gasped Frances, as though this was a very unusual thing indeed.

'Er, yeah. She used to work for a mail order company . . .' He hesitated, unsure if they would know what this was, but they seemed perfectly happy with the term. 'And Hamish, that's my stepdad, he's a travelling salesman.'

'Ah, he goes door-to-door, does he?' asked Frances.

'Well, more city-to-city, really. He sells shower fittings.'

'Goodness. It must take him an age to get between cities,' ventured Lou. 'Oh, no, he's got a good car . . . car . . . carpet,' stammered Tom.

Lou raised his eyebrows. 'A magic flying carpet, is it?' he asked. 'Like in *The Arabian Nights*? That would speed things up a bit.' He chuckled and looked at Lloyd, as though expecting him to join in, but Lloyd's face remained a picture of misery. Lou thought for a moment. 'What are shower fittings?' he asked.

'Oh, you know, like when you have a shower? The bits that . . . hold up the curtains and so forth.'

'Ah, in gymnasiums and public bathhouses,' ventured Lou.

'Er . . . yeah, sure.' Tom wasn't going to say that Hamish's shower fittings were used mostly in people's *homes*. Clearly, the Stevensons, like the rest of Edinburgh society, weren't quite ready for that idea.

'So . . . where exactly are your parents now?' asked Frances.

'Ah, well, they . . . they've gone away,' said Tom. 'Yeah. To the . . . the . . . South of France. On holiday.'

Lou looked puzzled. 'And they didn't take you with them?'

'Er . . . no, I . . . I thought they might like a bit of time on their own. You know, they haven't been together all that long and they're quite . . . lovey-dovey . . .'

Lou and Frances exchanged worried looks.

'And besides,' added Tom, 'I don't really get on all that well with my stepdad.'

Frances looked genuinely upset to hear that. 'Oh dear,' she said. 'What seems to be the problem?'

'Well, he's very changeable,' said Tom. 'One minute he's OK, the next, he's like some maniac. You know, a real Jekyll and Hyde.'

There was a long silence then and it occurred to Tom that they might not be familiar with the term. But then he thought about it and quickly realised why they *couldn't* be. Jekyll and Hyde was a description that lots of people used, but not everyone knew that it came from a book – a book by Robert Louis Stevenson; a book that he hadn't actually got around to writing yet.

'Jekyll . . . and Hyde?' murmured Lou.

'Umm . . . yeah, that's just something that people say. Around Manchester.'

'But what does it mean?'

'Oh, just that . . . some people, you know, they seem all meek and mild, but inside they're like . . . like . . .' He searched for inspiration and then an idea occurred to him. He pointed to the illustration on his t-shirt. 'A bit like this. They just hide behind this quite, normal look. But underneath it, they're like wild beasts.'

'That looks stupid,' said Lloyd, pointing a greasy knife at Tom's t-shirt.

'Lloyd,' said Frances quietly. 'What did I tell you before?'

Lou had a faraway look on his face. 'Imagine that,' he said, 'A quiet, respectable fellow. A man who shows the world a meek and mild exterior. A doctor perhaps, or a lawyer, trusted by everyone. But what if underneath, he's a raging animal, capable of the most appalling crimes?'

'Steady on,' said Tom. 'Hamish isn't *that* bad.' But inside he couldn't help feeling a thrill of exhilaration. Could it be . . . had he just given one of the world's greatest writers the idea for one of his most famous books? Judging by the look on Lou's face, ideas were already starting to form.

'You know, it's a bit like our old friend Deacon Brodie,' continued Lou. 'Deacon by day, burglar by night.' He looked at Tom. 'William Henley and I tried co-writing a play about him, but we can't seem to get it quite right. You're familiar with the man, I suppose?'

'Well, I've seen the pub,' said Tom. 'You know, the one on the Royal Mile? Where all the tourists . . .' His voice trailed off when he registered Lou's baffled expression.

'There's a pub?' muttered Lou.

'Oh, er . . . maybe I'm getting mixed up there. Yeah, I'm thinking of . . . er . . . a pub in Manchester.'

'There's a pub dedicated to Deacon Brodie in Manchester?' muttered Lou.

'So let me get this straight,' interrupted Frances. 'Your parents are travelling on the continent. But . . . they surely didn't leave you all on your own?'

'Oh, no, 'course not!' Tom realised that the Stevensons were looking at him intently and realised he needed to come up with something. He seized on the first Scottish name he could think of, one he remembered fondly from his last trip into the past. 'I'm staying with the − the McCallums.'

'Ah, a fine Edinburgh name,' observed Lou, coming out of his reverie. 'And which particular McCallums are they?'

'The, er . . . McCallums of Tanner's Close,' said Tom. 'Mary. Fraser. Catriona.'

Lou seemed to take great interest all of a sudden.

'Catriona McCallum?' he echoed. 'Not *the* Catriona McCallum?'

'Umm . . . maybe,' said Tom, warily.

'Well, I *know* a lady by that name. She's a very talented writer, as it happens. A member of a literary society I belong to. But . . . surely we can't be talking about the same person? She's quite elderly now. And she's never mentioned living on Tanner's Close. My God, isn't that where those terrible murders occurred back in the day? Burke and Hare! You know, I started writing a wee story based around them. I really must see about finishing it . . .'

But Tom was sitting there stunned. Realisation had hit him like a punch to the head, so powerfully, that he almost reeled backwards in his seat. It had never occurred to him that Catriona might still be alive. He'd last seen her as a middle-aged lady in a portrait in the National Museum of Scotland. Beneath it had been the dates of her birth and death. He couldn't recall them exactly, but he knew it was fifty-six years since his last visit here and she'd been around his age then, so it was quite possible.

'Catriona McCallum is still alive?' he croaked.

'Well, I should hope so, if you're staying with her,' said Frances. 'Tom, are you all right? You've gone quite pale.'

'I, sorry, I'm . . .' He pushed his plate aside, all thought of food forgotten. 'You know, I really should go and check in with her,' he said. 'She'll be worried.'

Lou and Frances looked disappointed, but Lloyd smiled delightedly at the idea of Tom leaving.

'Well, I hope you'll come back and visit us soon,' said Lou. 'You know, there's something about your company, Tom, that's quite . . . stimulating.'

'Thanks.' Tom got to his feet. 'And er . . . thanks for breakfast.' He caught Anna's eye and gave her the thumbs-up. 'Great scran,' he said. 'Seriously.' She looked helplessly at her employers as though seeking a translation.

Tom started backing towards the door.

'Your coat's hanging in the hallway,' Frances told him. 'Make sure you pick it up on your way through. It's cold out there.'

'I will, thanks. I'll catch you all later . . .' He paused as another thought occurred to him. 'One thing,' he said.

They looked at him expectantly. 'Yes?' murmured Lou.

'Catriona. Where exactly does she live?'

There was a long, perplexed silence. 'But . . . you're *staying* there,' reasoned Frances. 'So, surely . . .?'

'It's just gone right out of my head,' said Tom. He forced a laugh but nobody joined in. 'What am I like?' he asked them.

Lou and Frances exchanged glances. It was quite clear they didn't have the first idea what he was like. 'It's not far from here,' said Lou. '29, Lauriston Street. A rather grand house. You can't mistake it.' He frowned. 'Tom?'

'Yes?'

'We *are* going to see you again, aren't we?'

'Of course. Soon, I promise.'

And with that, he was out of the kitchen and hurrying

along the hallway to the front door, grabbing his overcoat on the way. He opened the door and stepped outside, shrugging the coat around him as he went. He descended the five steps, but as his foot connected with the pavement it seemed to grow soft beneath him, like a pool of warm oil, and his foot went right through it and into a blackness beyond. 'Oh no, not now!' he gasped. He tried to halt his own impetus but it was too late. He sank to the knees, to the waist, to the neck; and then the darkness enclosed him completely and as he fell further he heard again the brief fluttering of wings.

Six

Everything swam back into focus. He was standing in front of a familiar door: the door to Hamish's house in Fairmilehead. He felt a powerful sense of disappointment ripple through him. Why did he have to come back *now*, just when he'd found out that Cat was still alive? What if this new adventure was already over and he was back for good? Then he'd lost his chance of ever meeting her again.

He reached out to open the door and noticed something odd. It had been sparkling under fresh layers of red paint the last time he'd seen it, but now it looked weathered and battered. There was evidence of splintered wood around the lock as though it had been forced open at some point in the recent past. Tom frowned. He turned the handle, pushed the door open and stepped cautiously into the hallway.

The smell hit him first – the stale odour of dirt and decay. The hall carpet looked as though it hadn't seen a vacuum cleaner in months and over in one corner he saw what looked like a crumpled takeaway pizza box.

What was going on? Mum was always so houseproud and Hamish seemed to have gone along with that. Tom walked cautiously down to the open doorway of the living room, aware of the sounds of voices in there. Mum was sitting on the sofa with her back to him and she was watching the *Jonathan Guile* show. Now Tom knew that something really *was* wrong because Mum had always hated daytime TV, particularly this programme, a scurrilous talk show where hopeless members of the public were interrogated by the smug host and made to look like even bigger failures than they actually were.

'Mum, what's going . . .?' He broke off in surprise. On the TV screen, a woman was sitting slumped in a chair while Guile stood slightly to one side of her, clutching a clipboard. The woman was Mum. She was wearing a tatty green jumper and a pair of scruffy black leggings. Beside her, there was an empty seat, as though they were expecting somebody else.

OK, Tom told himself. *This kind of thing's happened before. It's an alternate reality. Just stay calm.*

But it was hard to do that when a caption flashed up on the screen. *My partner is an alcoholic!*

'You're just in time,' said Mum, without looking up at him. 'It's only been on a few minutes.' She sighed. 'I wish I'd worn a nicer top, though.'

'What are you doing on *this* show?' muttered Tom. 'I thought you hated it.'

'I do,' she muttered. 'But something had to be done.' She shook her head. 'Those leggings have seen better days. And why didn't I wash my hair?'

On screen, Guile started up with his opening gambit. 'So, Catherine, what prompted you to come on the show?'

'My partner, Hamish,' said the onscreen Mum. She looked pale and thin, Tom thought and she was right about her hair, it hung lank and greasy around her face. 'He's so, unpredictable.'

'Unpredictable?' Guile by contrast, was immaculately suited, his glossy hair brushed neatly into place, his blue eyes sparkling like those of a crafty fox. 'That's surely not a crime, Catherine? We all like a bit of the unpredictable in our lives, don't we? Surely it just makes things more interesting?'

'Not the way he does it,' Mum assured him. 'One minute he's nice and sweet, he's telling me everything has changed and he's going to behave himself . . .'

Guile nodded, doing the sympathetic face.

'The next, he goes out on a bender with his workmates and he drinks himself insensible. Then he comes back like a . . . like a wild beast.'

'Oh, but surely after a hard day's work, a man has earned the right to have a couple of pints?' reasoned Guile.

'It's not just a couple,' said Mum. 'He drinks himself insensible. And then he has these awful mood swings.'

'So he's a bit of a Jekyll and Hyde?' suggested Guile and Mum nodded.

'Exactly, Jonathan.'

'And you're perfect, I suppose?' Guile sat on the steps in front of the stage and consulted his clipboard. 'Because, let me tell you Catherine, that's not the picture that's coming across here. Let me see now, you've been arrested for shoplifting . . . and you've had a caution after a fight in a restaurant. You sound like the ideal model for parenthood, don't you?'

'That's not fair!' protested Mum. 'The shoplifting thing was an accident. I, I forgot to pay for something, that's all.'

'Oh, you forgot. And why did you forget, Catherine? Was it because you'd had a few drinks yourself? One too many gin and tonics over lunch?'

'Hamish drove me to it!'

'They all say that. But what makes you so different to him?'

'I . . . I try to be better. He's promised me a thousand times he'll clean up his act and turn over a new leaf. And for a week or so he manages it. He's the perfect gentleman. Kind. Thoughtful. He buys me flowers, takes me out to restaurants, tells me how much he cares about me.'

Guile sighed. 'At the end of the day, isn't that what every woman wants, Catherine?'

'Yes, but . . . then he lapses. He goes out with his friends again and he gets drunk. Horribly drunk and then . . .'

'Tell me, Catherine? Truthfully. Has he ever hit you?'

Mum lowered her head and muttered something.

'I'm sorry, I didn't quite catch that.'

'Yes! Yes, he hits me.'

'And how do you *feel* about that?'

She glared at him. 'How do you suppose I feel?

Scared, angry, humiliated . . . but that's not the worst of it. It's the way he treats my son, Tom.'

Tom moved to stand at the back of the sofa, intrigued.

'What do you mean?' asked Guile. 'Is he violent towards your son?'

Again, Mum nodded. 'Sometimes. And other times, he's just plain mean.'

'Give me an example.'

'Well, since Tom came up from Manchester to live with us, the two of them haven't really been getting along.'

'When did Tom move in with you?'

'A few months ago. Tom's father has a new partner, you see and, well, he made it clear that he didn't want Tom around any more, cramping his style.'

'He sounds like a charmer,' sneered Guile.

'It hit Tom really hard to be elbowed out like that. Him and his dad, they've always been so close. Anyway, the Christmas before it happened, Tom's dad bought him a Kindle.'

'Trying to buy him off, eh?' Guile turned to look at the audience. 'It's funny how many parents think they can do that, isn't it? But a fancy toy is no substitute for a loving parent.' He turned back. 'How old is Tom?'

'He's fourteen.'

'Ah, I remember being that age myself.' Guile glanced towards the camera. 'Back in the middle ages,' he added. Laughter swelled from the audience. He waited for it to die away before he said, 'Go on.'

'Well, one night Hamish came back from the pub and he was . . . absolutely off his head with drink. Even worse than usual and that's saying something.'

'And what about you, Catherine? Were you stone cold sober?'

'Yes, I was, actually.'

'Bully for you. Go on.'

'Well, Tom was just sitting there reading quietly, you know, trying to keep a low profile, because he *knows* how Hamish can be and Hamish started in on him. Told him that he should get out in the fresh air, play a game of football. He said he hated eBooks, thought they were the reason why so many children were failing their exams and, oh, all kinds of nonsense. None of it made any sense. Tom just tried to ignore him, and the more he did that, the angrier Hamish became until . . .'

'Until, what?'

'Until something snapped. He, oh, he . . .'

'Go on, Catherine. Tell me what he did.'

'He snatched the Kindle out of Tom's hands and he just stamped on it, over and over again. Smashed it into little bits. Tom just sat there and watched.'

Tom – the real Tom, reacted to that. 'Hamish broke my Kindle?' he cried and came around the side of the sofa. Mum looked up at him, puzzled.

'You *know* he did,' she said, but Tom barely registered the reply. He was too busy staring at her face. A big, purple bruise extended from the socket of her left eye to her cheek.

'Mum!' Tom promptly forgot to keep himself detached from what was happening and threw himself down on the sofa beside her. 'Did Hamish do this?' he demanded, reaching out and gently touching her face.

'Of course he did. He found out . . .'

'What?'

'That I'd been putting some housekeeping money aside each week to buy you a new Kindle. He was like a madman.'

'Where is he?' snarled Tom.

'He's upstairs, sleeping it off.' Tom started to get up, but Mum grabbed his arm and pulled him down again. 'Don't go up there,' she advised him. 'Please. Let him sober up a bit. If you wake him now, he'll only start on us again. Besides, you'll miss the rest of the show. I'm recording this, I hope I can get Hamish to watch it with me when he's sobered up.'

Tom frowned, not particularly caring about the programme, but Mum hung tightly onto him, so he settled back and put a protective arm around her shoulders.

Onscreen, Guile was back on his feet and grandstanding to his audience, striding up and down the stage like some Roman emperor. 'So what do we think, ladies and gentlemen?' he cried. 'Does Hamish sound like a nice guy? Or does he sound like a five star, solid gold creep?' There was a roar of agreement from the studio audience. The camera panned around them, showing their angry faces. They were waving their fists at the stage and yelling for Hamish's blood.

'Do we think this man should be allowed to carry on in the same manner? Or should he be brought to account for his actions?'

Another concerted shout from the crowd.

'Shall we get him out here?'

Now they were positively howling their indignation.

Guile stood for a moment, looking left and right, a smug little smile on his face.

'All right, would you please welcome to the stage – Hamish!'

A stunned silence descended as a figure came gliding out from the wings, a tall, thin figure dressed in a full-length leather cape and gauntlets, his face hidden behind a crow-like leather mask with a huge curved beak. He took a seat beside Mum, who was staring at him in astonishment. She appeared to be frozen in position.

The camera closed in on Guile. He looked outraged. There was some uncertain laughter from the crowd.

'What's with the fancy dress?' he demanded.

But there was no response from the figure in the seat. The newcomer just stared back at Guile through round red goggles.

Guile turned to gaze imploringly at his audience.

'What do we think, ladies and gentlemen? We invite a man to come on our show and *this* is how he turns up? Does this strike you as respectful?'

'NO!' roared the crowd.

'Do we think he's treating this process with the dignity it deserves?'

'NO,' repeated the crowd.

'Should I have it out with him?'

'YES!'

Guile turned and strode towards the masked figure. 'I don't ask for very much,' he said. 'A little politeness. Some basic good manners. And when I invite somebody to appear on my programme, I expect them to at least have the decency to show me their face.' With that he leaned forward, took hold of the top of the mask and yanked it upwards, revealing the face beneath.

Tom felt a jolt of terror go through him. Because McSweeny's head was just a skull with the occasional scrap of shrivelled flesh attached to it, all that was left of him after the quicklime had done its work. On the sofa beside Tom, Mum – the real Mum – gave a gasp of revulsion and clutched at Tom's arm.

'I don't understand,' she whispered. 'This isn't what happened.'

Guile was slow to react. He appeared to be about to take a step back, but in that same instant McSweeny's gloved right hand shot out and clamped tight around Guile's throat. Then McSweeny stood, lifting the talk show host bodily off the ground as though he weighed no more than a bundle of clothing. Guile's skinny legs kicked wildly as he struggled to free himself. McSweeny took a couple of steps closer to the audience and then, almost contemptuously, he tossed Guile straight into their midst. The camera cut to a shot of the audience, people screaming and scrambling out of their seats in a panic as Guile crashed amongst them in an ungainly sprawl. Now the camera cut back to the stage, where Mum had finally realised that she needed to move. She jumped up out of her seat, but McSweeny stepped quickly back and, grabbing a handful of her hair, he pulled her to him.

'Don't be in such a hurry, Catherine,' he croaked in that familiar rasping voice. He slipped an arm around her waist and pulled her with him across the stage as he strode closer to the camera. His empty eye sockets stared out of the screen and as he began to talk Tom's blood turned to ice within him.

'Tom! I know you can see me. Look what you did to me. Look!' His hideous fleshless face filled the screen. 'I have no eyes, but I can see you. I have no nose, but I can smell you. I have no tongue but I can taste you. I'm coming for you, boy. Do you hear me? I'm coming to get you. And there's nowhere you can hide from me. Nowhere.'

Beside him, Mum let out a snuffling little cry. The camera pulled back to reveal her terrified face. She was gasping for breath as the adrenalin pumped through her. 'Now,' crooned McSweeny. 'What shall we do with your dear mother? Do you remember what happened to my mother, Tom? Thrown into a jail and left to rot, and all because of you. So, shall we finish it quickly? Or shall we take our own sweet time about it?'

'Tom, Tom, turn it off!' cried Mum, cowering beside him on the sofa.

Tom obeyed instinctively. He couldn't see the remote control, so he ran across to the television as McSweeny continued to rant. 'Shall I make her feel the pain you caused me, boy? Shall I burn the very flesh from her bones?'

Tom reached for the off switch.

And a gloved hand burst out of the television and grabbed him by the throat with a power that made him wince. It began to pull him slowly towards the screen. Tom tried frantically to hit the off button, but McSweeny's arm was blocking his view and in his panic he couldn't seem to locate it. The hand around his throat was tightening, cutting off his air supply. His head filled with a buzzing red mist. Now his face was moving towards the screen, but the glass seemed to melt as his forehead touched it and then he was being pulled into the television, while manic laugher exploded all around him.

'Welcome home, Tom,' crooned that hateful voice.

And blackness descended once again.

Seven

Tom opened his eyes to find himself enclosed in a swaying, clattering semi-darkness. A sour-looking face was peering closely at him, as though searching for signs of life. He recognised Lloyd's glum little features. 'He's awake,' announced Lloyd, sounding far from happy at the news.

He was back in Edinburgh. The thought barely registered because by now he was very used to the practise of flying around in time and space. Another face swam into focus. Lou. He was looking at Tom in the gloom, his expression anxious. 'Are you all right, old sport?' he asked.

Tom registered a smell of leather and horse and realised that he was in a hansom cab, but this time he was at least comfortably seated. Through a narrow gap in the window blind to his left, he saw that the vehicle was making its way noisily along cobbled streets, the horse's iron-shod hooves rattling out a fearsome tattoo. Tom didn't have the least idea how he'd got here but again, he no longer really questioned such things.

'You were making noises in your sleep,' said Lloyd and managed to make it sound like a terrible accusation. 'You were whimpering.'

'You've been sleeping a lot lately,' said Lou. 'More than seems natural. Do you know what's happening, Tom?'

'Umm . . .' He struggled to try and piece everything together. 'The last thing I remember is . . . is leaving your house to go and see . . .' It came back to him in a rush. 'Catriona!' he said. He sat up. 'Did I, did I get to see her?'

Lou shook his head. 'You barely got three steps outside the door,' he said. 'Two minutes after you left us the doorbell rang and a stranger reported that you'd collapsed on the pavement. Sleeping like the dead, you were.'

'We thought you were dead,' said Lloyd, sounding rather disappointed that they'd been wrong.

'Of course, we summoned a doctor,' said Lou. 'He examined you and said he thought that you were suffering from nervous exhaustion. He advised us to put you to bed, which is mostly where you've been for the past two days. But this morning, you got up and had breakfast, bright as a lark.'

'I did?'

'Yes. And when I suggested you might accompany Lloyd and myself on this little errand tonight, you said you thought it was a capital idea. Don't you remember any of that?'

'Erm, I . . . er . . .' Tom tried to gather together any images from the last couple of days but failed miserably. 'No, not really,' he admitted. 'I do get these blanks from time to time. I'm not sure why.'

'As soon as we climbed into the coach, you were gone again,' said Lloyd. 'And then you started making strange noises . . .'

'All right, son.' Lou gave Lloyd a sharp look. He turned back to Tom. 'I'm beginning to think that it's something more serious than just exhaustion. How do you feel now?'

'I feel . . . okay,' said Tom, and he wasn't lying. Despite the brief return to his own time, he felt calm, rested. His mum's appearance on the *Jonathan Guile* show seemed nothing more than a bad dream he'd had. And perhaps that's all it had been. 'So, where exactly are we going?' he asked.

'To visit Long John Silver,' said Lou, with a grin.

'Oh, right, your friend? The one you said you based the character on?'

'Correct,' finished Lou. 'I've decided to take your advice and press him to pester his publishing colleagues to have a wee look at *Treasure Island*. I'm counting on you, Tom, to help me convince him that it's an idea worth trying.'

'Well, I'll give it a go,' said Tom.

'Me too, Papa!' said Lloyd urgently. '*I'll* help you.'

'Of course you will.' Lou patted the boy's head fondly, then looked at Tom again and his expression became grave. 'Tom, there's something we need to talk about. When we found you unconscious, I sent a messenger around to Miss McCallum's house. Naturally, I wanted to assure her that you were well and under our protection.' He shook his head.

'What is it?' asked Tom, anxiously. 'Has something happened to Cat? I mean, Miss McCallum?'

'No. Well, not so far as I'm aware, anyway. Her manservant said that she was out of the country for a few days. In England, as it happens, doing a series of lectures. She'll be back the day after tomorrow. Christmas Eve.'

'Oh, well that's a relief,' said Tom.

'Perhaps, but it does suggest that you haven't been entirely truthful with us. You said you were staying with Miss McCallum, isn't that right?'

'Er, yeah . . .'

'But the manservant denied all knowledge of you.'

'Oh,' said Tom. 'I see. Well, I am a good friend of Catriona's but I haven't seen her for quite a while. She doesn't know I'm back yet.'

'You said you were *staying* with her.'

'I meant, I was *going* to stay with her.'

'So she doesn't know about it yet?'

'No, not yet, but don't worry, we're good mates, me and Cat.'

'You're a dirty liar,' said Lloyd.

'Lloyd,' snapped Lou. 'That is not a nice word.'

'It's true though,' protested Lloyd.

'Quiet, son,' said Lou. 'Let's see what Tom has to say for himself before we go jumping to conclusions.' He stared at Tom. 'Go on.'

Tom considered his options. He supposed he could try telling Lou the truth, though Tom wasn't sure he was quite ready for that yet. Or he could make something up. After a moment's hesitation, he opted for the latter.

'The thing is,' he said, 'I've, I've run away from home.'

'I see,' said Lou, gravely. 'Is this because of your stepfather? The . . . heckle and snide character.'

'Jekyll and Hyde,' Tom corrected him and thought how weird it was. After all, it was, or at least it *would* be, one of Lou's books, at some point in the not-too-distant future. He made a mental note to keep mentioning it regularly, just to make sure the title stuck.

'You're saying this Hamish character is violent towards you?'

'Well, not exactly. But he's really sarky, sometimes. *And* he's a Hibs fan.'

'A what?'

'Oh, it's a . . .'

'You mean, the football team? Hibernian?'

'Oh, yeah. Are they . . . already going?'

'Irishmen. They play down in Leith, I believe. Quite a new club. I don't really follow the sport, but I believe they're closely identified with the Irish Home Rule Movement.'

'Is that right?' Tom was astonished. 'Wow.'

He had no idea that a football club would have such a long history. 'Well, anyway, Hamish follows them and, and he drinks a lot, too.' He felt vaguely guilty saying this, after the seemingly reformed Hamish he had recently encountered, but he supposed he had to say *something* that would explain his situation. 'So I thought, I know, I'll run away from home and I'll stay with my old mate, Cat, er, Catriona.'

Lou looked worried. 'Well, it's very irregular,' he said. 'It seems to me you'll have to furnish me with your parent's address in Fairmilehead. I'll write to them and explain that you're staying with us as a guest. Then we'll see what they propose to do about it.'

That could be interesting, thought Tom. *Don't expect a quick reply.* But he didn't say anything.

'You know, son,' continued Lou, 'running away from a problem is really not the best way to deal with it.'

'No,' agreed Tom. 'I understand.'

'You need to be a man about it,' said Lloyd, as though he had considerable experience of the subject. 'You need to look your problems in the eye and deal with them.' He was obviously repeating something that his father, the 'Civil War hero' had told him. Lloyd allowed himself a smug smile and Tom felt like blowing a big loud raspberry in his face.

'We won't let it cloud the evening,' announced Lou. 'Let's talk about it when we're home.' He leaned back in his seat. 'But Tom, there's something else I wanted to ask you.'

'Oh yeah?' Tom looked at him warily. 'What's that, then?'

'Do you *really* know Catriona McCallum?'

Tom stared at him. 'Yeah, of course,' he said.

'You see, I've always found her very hard to approach. She strikes me as an extremely interesting lady, one who has evidently led a colourful life. But on the few occasions I've had the opportunity to speak to her, she's barely given me the time of day.'

'Oh, well, I've known her for ages,' said Tom. 'Yeah,

we used to knock around together. We were almost like . . . boyfriend and girlfriend.'

Lou stared at him. 'But, she's in her seventies,' he said.

'Umm . . .'

There was a deep silence. Tom sat there, trying to think of something to say, but the life of him he couldn't come up with anything.

Then a hearty 'whoah!' from the coachman announced that they had arrived at their destination. Relieved at the diversion, Tom opened the door of the cab and leapt quickly out. He turned back to help Lou step down and saw that the cab had stopped outside a grand terrace of three storey town houses. Lloyd jumped out and slammed the door shut. Lou turned back to speak to the driver who was sitting up at the rear of the compartment.

'Come back for us at eleven o' clock,' he said. The cab driver nodded. He was cloaked against the bitter cold. A scarf was pulled across the lower part of his face and a broad-brimmed hat pulled down over his eyes. He cracked his whip and rode away.

Lou turned back and gave Tom a shrewd look. 'Don't think I'll forget to ask you that question again,' he murmured. 'Because your story does not make any kind of sense.' He stepped past the boys and led the way up the stone steps to a huge, black painted door. 'Now,' he said, looking at his companions. 'The charm offensive begins.'

And with that he reached out and rang the bell.

Eight

William Henley was standing in front of a marble fireplace when the visitors were ushered into his front room. Lit by the flames of a roaring fire, his tall burly figure instantly displayed how he had inspired the character of Long John Silver. He was a big, broad-shouldered fellow with handsome features and an unruly red beard that hung down onto his chest. He was resting his weight on a simple wooden crutch and Tom could see that his left leg finished at the knee, where his trousers were neatly folded back and secured. As his guests approached, he grinned delightedly at them.

'Here he is at last,' he said, in a big, booming voice, with what Tom immediately recognised as a cultured English accent. 'Edinburgh's most intriguing author and his little Yankee chip-off-the-old-block.' He prodded Lloyd in the chest with a huge index finger, making him squirm. 'I was beginning to think you two had abandoned me to my own poor company.' He transferred his attention to Tom. 'But who the devil's this? You didn't tell me you were bringing someone else!'

'This is Tom Afflick,' said Lou. 'A . . . new acquaintance. I hope you'll forgive me, I took the liberty of bringing him along. He came to my aid the other night when I was suffering from a spot of the old trouble and helped me to get home. He's er, staying with us for a few days.'

'Is he now?'

'Yes, he is,' muttered Lloyd glumly and Lou shot him a warning glance.

'Well, I'm delighted to meet you, young Tom.' William extended a meaty hand and pumped Tom's arm vigorously up and down. 'Any friend of the Stevensons is a friend of mine.' He took a step back, moving with practised ease on the wooden crutch. 'The season's greetings to you all, I'm sure!'

'And to you also, William,' said Lou. He looked with evident envy at the tall, richly decorated tree standing in the corner of the room, it's topmost plume nearly touching the high ceiling. 'I must say your tree puts our puny effort well and truly to shame.'

William rolled his eyes. 'Oh, you know Hannah. Every year, the blessed thing seems to grow bigger and more luxurious. I'm not as convinced of these strange German customs as she is. But, I suppose if it's good enough for our dear Queen, then it shall do for me.'

Lou looked around the room. 'And where *is* Hannah?' he enquired.

'Alas, she had some infernal matter to attend to at her parents. But, as I already knew that Fran wouldn't be accompanying you, I didn't dissuade Hannah from staying with them for the night. I thought we'd have a lads' evening,' he added, with a sly wink. 'But come, come, I'm forgetting my manners! A glass of malt whisky would I'm sure be agreeable, Lou. And perhaps some cordial for the two younger members of the party?'

'I'd like to try the whisky,' said Lloyd, bluntly.

'I'm sure you would,' said Lou, calmly. 'But it'll be cordial for you for a few years yet, Sonny Jim.'

Servants were summoned, drinks were brought on silver trays and then they all seated themselves comfortably around the fire. Tom found himself sitting, much to Lloyd's evident annoyance, right next to Lou.

'So,' said William, smiling at Lou. 'It is of course, always a pleasure to see such a dear friend, but the tone of your note rather suggested that you had some particular reason in wanting to see me.'

Lou nodded. 'I trust you'll forgive me, William, and I know how dreary it is to have to discuss business when you're supposed to be relaxing . . .'

William waved a hand in dismissal. 'Not at all,' he said. 'Come along, out with it. What's on your mind?'

'Well, I've been discussing *The Sea Cook*, with Tom here . . .'

'*Treasure Island*,' Tom corrected him.

'*The Wreck of the Hispaniola*,' added Lloyd.

'Er, quite. And I've come to the conclusion that perhaps the pages of the *Young Folks* paper is not the best place for it.'

William frowned. 'I see. Am I to take it that you're not happy with the terms of your contract with Mr Henderson?'

'Oh, no, it's nothing like that,' said Lou hastily. 'He has

been most accommodating. And of course I'm grateful to Dr Jap for introducing me to him in the first place. But, well, Henderson's last letter suggested that the serial hasn't been so well received by readers of the paper. In fact, he intimated to me that sales were slightly down on previous editions.'

William scowled. 'Well, there's no accounting for taste,' he said. 'For my part, I think it's a splendid story. Full of swashbuckling adventure.'

'I think it has its charms,' said Lou. 'I'll admit, I had thought that it would travel no further than the pages of a halfpenny periodical, but Tom here . . .'

William looked at Tom with interest. 'What about him?'

'He thinks it's destined for bigger things. And, well, I'm afraid he's rather persuaded me to pursue the idea of releasing it as a . . . as a book.'

William smiled. 'I see.' He looked at Tom with interest. 'And what makes you think that's such a good idea?' he asked.

Tom was aware that everyone was looking at him, most of them fondly, but in Lloyd's case with venom virtually shooting out of his eyes.

'Well, I, I've *read* it, obviously.'

'Not *all* of it,' William reminded him. 'There's still quite a few more instalments to come, isn't that right, Lou?'

'Yes. It runs through till late January.'

Tom nodded. He remembered that he was only half way through the book version himself, but he wasn't going to let that put him off. 'Erm, right. But from what I have read . . . I just think it's a brilliant book that's got a really big future ahead of it.'

'You have a crystal ball, do you?' asked William.

'Sort of,' admitted Tom. 'You know when you just have a feeling about something? When you just kind of . . . *know*?'

'Well, that's not to be sneezed at,' observed William. 'Gut reactions are as good as any other method when trying to deduce the potential of a story. As I was only saying to James Barrie, the other day, one must . . .'

Tom wondered why that name was vaguely familiar to him and his puzzled look must have been evident.

'He's one of William's young cronies,' said Lou. 'I believe the lad has ideas about becoming a playwright, isn't that right, William?'

William nodded. 'He's a smashing young fellow, actually. Studying literature at the University at the moment. He wanted to try and be a writer, but his parents persuaded him that there was no security in it and urged him to get a degree. Mind you, in his spare time, he's writing drama reviews for the *Edinburgh Evening News* under the name, J.M. Barrie. Anyway, he was asking me only the other day . . .'

'J.M. Barrie?' asked Tom incredulously. 'Isn't that, I'm sorry, isn't that the guy who wrote *Peter Pan*?'

Lou and William looked at him in puzzlement.

'I don't recall anything by that name,' said William. 'As I say, he's really only starting out, it's reviews and short pieces mostly. But he does have an ambition to write for the stage one day.' He waved a hand in dismissal. 'We were having lunch the other day and he asked me what I thought would make the perfect subject for a successful play. I said to him, James, you simply have to go with your gut reaction.'

Tom shook his head. 'Just tell him to write about a kid who never grew up,' he said, and then became aware that the others were giving him very odd looks indeed. 'I mean, it's just an idea,' he muttered. 'Off the top of my head.' He felt vaguely stunned and wondered how many other famous authors were lurking in the shadows of Edinburgh. He half-expected another one to leap out from behind the Christmas tree at any moment and start handing out copies of his latest bestseller.

William smiled. 'Anyway, enough about young James and his lofty ambitions. It's Lou we're discussing at the moment, somebody who has already made his mark upon the literary world. And I suppose what you're asking me is, do I think that *The Sea Cook* . . .?'

'*Treasure Island*,' said Tom.

'*The Wreck of the Hispaniola!*' snapped Lloyd

'Er . . . indeed. Do I think the story could reach a wider audience?' William appeared to consider for a moment. 'Well, one must bear in mind, of course, that it *is* only aimed at younger readers, so . . .'

'That's a *huge* audience,' Tom assured him. 'Massive. Every school in the country will want to have that as a class reader.'

William seemed amused by this. 'You seem to know quite a bit about the publishing industry,' he observed. 'Are you from that background yourself?

Your parents perhaps or . . .?'

'No! No, I'm just . . .'

'He's just a know-all,' murmured Lloyd and once again, received a warning glare from Lou.

William ignored the comment. 'Well, clearly, Lou, you'll have to wait at least until the serial has run its course, before you can even *think* of offering it to someone else. I seem to remember you telling me that your contract with Mr Henderson was only for first publication rights. The copyright remains with you, is that correct?'

'That's what I understand to be the case,' agreed Lou.

'Then there's nothing to be done just yet.'

Lou seemed disappointed. 'You think not?'

'Lou, you mustn't be impatient. The world of publishing goes to sleep at this time of year and never properly wakes up again until the spring. But rest assured, my friend, when the time seems favourable, I shall certainly write some letters to contacts of mine in London. We'll see if some of them might at least cast a critical eye over the manuscript.'

'And I, in the meantime, shall undertake a few revisions,' said Lou. 'Just to ensure it is every bit as good as it can be.'

'Capital!' William beamed. 'Well, then,' he said. 'Let's drink to its success, shall we?' He lifted his glass of whisky. *'The Sea Cook,'* he said.

Tom lifted his cordial. *'Treasure Island,'* he insisted.

Lloyd lifted his glass and opened his mouth to say something, but must have noted the glares he was getting from both Tom and Lou. He sighed, scowled, and shrugged his narrow shoulders. 'To *Treasure Island*,' he muttered and they all drank.

Nine

They sat and chatted and enjoyed their drinks which were replenished at regular intervals and eventually it grew late. Lou pulled a pocket watch from his waistcoat and announced that the hansom cab they'd booked would be arriving presently. They said their goodbyes to William and trooped out to the hallway, where servants were waiting to help them on with their coats. A maid opened the front door and sure enough, there was the cab, gliding to a halt in the dull glow of the gas lamps, the driver sitting up at the rear of the vehicle, heavily cloaked and hooded against the cold.

'You two go ahead and get in,' suggested Lou. 'I just remembered something else.' He turned back to have a last word with William who had come to the door to wave them off. 'Before I forget, William, Tom told me that our old friend Deacon Brodie has had a pub named after him in Manchester, of all places!'

'Really?' William looked incredulous at this news. 'I'm often there and I've never seen it. Whereabouts is it?'

Tom hastily led Lloyd across the pavement to the cab, anxious to avoid any more awkward questions. He reached up and opened the door, then waited politely while Lloyd got his skinny frame inside. Tom climbed in and settled himself on the seat opposite the boy.

'I'm tired,' complained Lloyd. 'I wish Papa would hurry up.'

'I'm sure he won't be long,' said Tom. It occurred to him then that the driver hadn't spoken a word to them, so he tilted back his head to look at the closed hatch above him. 'Mr Stevenson will just be a minute,' he shouted.

There was no reply. Indeed, the silence was so deep and so intense, that Tom suddenly had a powerful sense of foreboding. He made a move towards the open door of the cab, meaning to lean out and repeat the instruction, but at that moment it slammed shut in his face with a force that almost made him jump out of his skin. In the same instant, he heard a deep voice bellow, 'Hah!' There was the crack of a whip and the cab leapt forward with a suddenness that made Tom rock back in his seat.

Through the window, he caught a glimpse of a bemused Lou, turning on the doorstep in surprise to look towards the cab as it sped away from the house, but an instant later the window blind shot downwards with what seemed like supernatural speed, cutting off Tom's view entirely. A lock engaged with a loud clunk. 'What the—? Hey, hold on a minute,' bellowed Tom. 'Wait for Mr Stevenson, he's coming with us!'

Again there was no answer. If anything, the speed

of the cab increased, the fragile vehicle shuddering and shaking over the cobbles as though about to fall to pieces. Again, Tom heard the sound of a whip cracking on the frozen air and the coachman's hoarse voice shouted, 'Giddy up!'

And Tom knew something was terribly wrong because that voice was all too familiar.

Lloyd's pale features stared at him in the gloom. 'What's going on?' he cried. 'Why aren't we waiting for Papa?'

Tom didn't know what to tell him. He reached out to the blind and tried to unlatch it, but it seemed somehow clamped to the glass and he could get no more than a peek around the side of it at the rows of houses flashing by them as the horse, spurred on by the whip, stretched itself into a full gallop.

Then the hatch above them slid back with a loud thud and a hideous face peered triumphantly down at them, a grinning skull that seemed to emanate a dull, malevolent glow. 'Hello Tom!' cried a familiar rasping voice. 'Welcome back to Edinburgh!'

Lloyd stared up in goggle-eyed amazement for a moment and then began to scream, high and shrill, like a bird.

McSweeny cackled in delight. 'And you've brought a wee friend along for the ride!' he roared. 'How splendid!'

The hatch slid shut again and Tom sat there, numb with shock, in the bucketing, clattering cab, telling himself that he mustn't panic, that there was a way out of this, there *had* to be. But Lloyd was still shrieking dementedly and Tom couldn't think straight, couldn't pull his scattered thoughts together.

Almost without thinking, he reached out and slapped Lloyd hard, across the face. Even in the midst of such panic he was astonished to register how satisfying it felt. Lloyd fell abruptly silent. He slumped back in his seat and sat there, staring at Tom open-mouthed.

'What was that for?' he whined.

'I need to think,' Tom assured him.

'But, I . . .'

'Shush!'

Above him, he heard McSweeny's voice as it broke into a tuneless song.

'What'll we do with the herring's heads?
The herring's heads, the herring's heads?
Make them into loaves of bread
And all sorts of things.
Of all the fish that swim in the sea
The herring is the one for me . . .'

Tom cursed. He grabbed the handle of the cab's door and struggled to twist it open but couldn't make it budge. So he shifted around onto his backside and launched a kick at the lock, putting all his strength behind it and sending a shudder up the entire length of his spine. The door remained resolutely shut.

'What are you doing?' cried Lloyd. 'You'll damage the door!'

'I'm trying to get it open,' Tom told him. 'Don't just sit there like an idiot, give me a hand!'

'But . . . who is that?' gasped Lloyd, pointing upwards.

Tom ignored the question and lashed another kick at the door. The varnished wood seemed to buckle a little, but the lock held fast.

What'll we do with the herring's eyes?
The herring's eyes, the herring's eyes?
Make them into puddings and pies.
And all sorts of things
Of all the fish that swim in the sea,
The herring is the one for me!

Tom suddenly had a terrible thought. Why was McSweeny singing about *fish*? He swung around, clambered up onto the seat and grabbing the handle of the hatch, he slid it open and pushed his head through, cringing because he knew that McSweeny's hideous figure was only inches behind him. A foul smell filled his nostrils, a stench of decay that almost made him gag, but he steeled himself and looked in the direction the coach was heading. He saw that it was racing along a narrow street that plunged steeply downhill. Several hundred yards further on there was a stone wharf which ended suddenly in a sheer drop to the river below. Tom's eyes bulged. He tried to drop down again but a gloved hand closed around the back of his neck, holding him in place. He could feel the deadly grip of bare bones beneath the leather gauntlet.

'What's the big hurry, Tom?' snarled a voice in his ear. 'Don't you fancy a wee swim? Are ye not in the mood?'

Tom made a supreme effort and wrenched himself free, tearing tufts of hair from the back of his neck in the process. He yelped, dropped onto the seat and twisted around onto his back again. Lloyd sat there, staring open-mouthed at him as he renewed his efforts, pounding both feet repeatedly against the lock, putting all his strength into the task. The door buckled a little more, but continued to hold as he kicked and kicked, sweating profusely in the cramped interior of the coach.

'What are you *doing*?' screamed Lloyd, but Tom ignored him, horribly aware that time was fast running out. He gave one last kick, putting everything he had left into it and this time the door smashed crazily open, tore itself from its hinges and tumbled away, revealing the sight of grey stone tenements blurring past as the coach gathered pace for the final push. The whip cracked again and above them McSweeny was laughing dementedly. Tom looked at Lloyd. 'We have to jump,' he yelled.

Lloyd seemed to shrink down in his seat. 'No,' he said, shaking his head. 'I won't. You can't make me.'

'We *have* to!' insisted Tom, but the boy was having none of it, so Tom grabbed him around the waist and pulled him headlong towards the door. Lloyd began to struggle, kicking his legs, shaking his head from side to side.

'No,' he gasped, 'no, NO!'

Tom somehow got him to the very edge of the door, aware as he did so that they had left the last houses behind and were entering the final empty space that bordered the wharf. 'Do you want to drown?' he bellowed.

Lloyd froze, staring back at him in the shuddering, bucketing gloom and that was when Tom made his move, rising to his feet and throwing the two of them out through the doorway, trying to ensure that he got them clear of the coach's rear wheels as it sped past. As they fell, Tom thought he heard a yell from above him, a great howl of frustration as McSweeny registered that once again, Tom had eluded him.

The two boys seemed to fall for a very long time. Tom anticipated pain as they hit the cobbles but miraculously, a pile of full sacks intervened, deadening their fall. As they landed in a sprawl of arms and legs, Tom turned his head and saw the coach racing on, passing over the edge of the wharf and then the horse, the cab and McSweeny hurtled downwards, hit the grey surface of the river in a great splash of foam and disappeared from sight.

Tom lay for a moment, trying to get his breath back. Then he struggled upright, pulling Lloyd with him. 'Come on,' he said. 'We need to run.'

'But . . . the cab, it . . .'

'He won't be dead!' screamed Tom.

'He went in the water. He must have drowned.'

'Nothing kills him. Nothing! Do you understand? Now, come on.' He began to run back along the street and Lloyd, clearly terrified, ran after him. They pounded uphill, running for all they were worth and they kept going until they were both out of breath and were finally obliged to slow to a walk, but even then

Tom wasn't going to stop. He led the way onwards, throwing occasional glances back down the hill, but thankfully, nothing seemed to be following them.

'What?' gasped Lloyd. 'What happened back there? Who . . . *what*, was that thing?'

'An old friend,' murmured Tom.

'A friend?' Lloyd looked bewildered. 'He, he tried to kill us.'

'They don't get much past you,' said Tom, acidly. His mind was whirling as he tried to decide what to do. It was clear he was going to have to level with Lloyd, much as he hated the idea. There simply didn't seem to be any other choice and he realised he had to work fast, before the two of them were reunited with Lou. He looked at the boy. 'All right,' he said. 'I'll explain everything, but you'll have to listen until I've finished talking.'

'But . . .'

'I mean it Lloyd. Are you going to listen?'

Lloyd scowled, but he nodded.

'All right,' said Tom. 'It all began in a place called Mary King's Close, in the year 2013.'

As they walked he told Lloyd, as briefly as he could, everything that had happened to him since his first trip into the past. To give the boy his due he did listen carefully to every word, but the shifting expressions on his face ranged from doubtful to downright disbelieving. When Tom had finally got to the end of his story, he looked at Lloyd and shrugged his shoulders. 'Well, that's about it,' he said. 'What do you think?'

Lloyd scowled, which seemed to be his default expression. 'You're saying that you're . . . from the future?' he muttered.

'Yes. I know how it sounds, but . . . well, that's how I know that your dad is going to be one of the most famous writers in history. That book he's written?'

'*The Wreck of the Hispaniola*?'

'Don't start! *Treasure Island*! It's going to be read for hundreds of years. It's going to become a children's classic. On the way to Edinburgh, I was reading that book. But not on paper. I was using an electronic book, a kind of little box that can hold thousands of stories—' He broke off as Lloyd gave a grunt of exasperation and on reflection Tom had to admit that it *did* sound pretty unbelievable. He pointed back down the street. 'That man – or what's left of him – has been chasing me ever since I first came back in time. Don't tell me he's not real, because you've *seen* him, you've seen what he can do.'

Lloyd sighed. 'I've seen him,' he agreed. 'And I really wish I hadn't.'

'The thing is, Lloyd, this is going to have to be our secret.'

Lloyd glared at him. 'But why?' he demanded. 'I tell my parents everything that happens to me.'

'I get that, I really do. But see . . .' Tom struggled to think of a way he could explain it. 'Time is like . . . it's like, you know, dominoes?'

Lloyd looked puzzled. 'The game? The little black squares?'

'Yeah. Well, you must have done that thing, right,

where you line them all up and you knock one over? And they all fall down, one after the other, even if the line goes for miles and miles?'

Lloyd grinned, nodded. 'Of course,' he said. 'Once I made a line that stretched from . . .'

'Never mind that now! Just think about it. Time is sort of like that row of dominoes. If we take out just one of them, the line is broken. And things will stop falling. So, like I said, your dad is going to be really famous. But only if he does the things he's supposed to do.'

Lloyd frowned. 'I don't understand,' he said.

'Well, remember what he said to Mr Henley before? That he was going to revise *Treasure Island* before he sends it out to the publishers? He really needs to do that if he wants to get it published as a book. But, if we turn up talking about time travel and . . . and plague doctors trying to kill us and mad stuff like that, he's going to get distracted, isn't he? The last thing he's going to think about is working on some book. So he won't bother making the changes. And that way, well, that way *Treasure Island* might never happen. Maybe it'll just stay as a serial in a kid's magazine and nobody will ever hear about it again.'

Lloyd looked crestfallen. 'You're saying Papa *isn't* going to be famous?'

'I'm saying he *might* not be. Not unless we help. And the best way to help is to keep quiet about what's happened and just encourage him to get on with those revisions. Because believe me, Lloyd, if he doesn't do them, you can kiss it all goodbye. And it will be your fault. ' He gave Lloyd a stern look. 'So it's up to you, mate.'

'But that's not fair,' protested Lloyd.

'Nobody said it had to be,' Tom assured him. He lifted his head at the sound of approaching hooves. Another hansom cab was rattling towards them from the other end of the street and a familiar face was leaning anxiously out of the window. Tom lifted a hand to wave. 'Remember,' he urged Lloyd. 'If you want everything to work out for your dad . . .'

'I understand,' muttered Lloyd, but he didn't look at all happy about it. Then he seemed to think of something. 'It works two ways though,' he said.

Tom glanced at him suspiciously. 'What do you mean?'

'I mean that I know all about you now. So if you want me to stay quiet about it, you're going to have to start doing what *I* say.'

'Oh, now look . . .'

'I mean it, Tom.' For the first time that night Lloyd was smiling, but it was a creepy, supercilious kind of smile. 'From now on, I say what happens. You have to do what I tell you. Deal?'

Tom sighed. He didn't like the idea but realised that he was in no position to argue. 'Deal,' he said.

Now the cab was pulling to a halt a short distance from them. The door opened and Lou jumped out. 'What in the name of heaven just happened?' he cried. 'It took me an age to find another cab. Are you two all right?'

'We're fine, Papa,' said Lloyd.

'Something must have spooked the other horse,' said Tom. 'The driver couldn't get it to stop.'

'My word!' Lou stared down the street. 'Where's the cab now?'

'It just kept going,' Tom assured him. 'So we . . . hopped out.'

Lou stared at him. 'You hopped out?' He shook his head. 'But the horse was going at a gallop. It looked to me as though the driver was using the whip!'

'Only to try and get it to stop,' Lloyd assured him.

'But that doesn't make sense!'

'That's what *we* thought,' Tom assured him. 'That's kind of why we hopped out.'

'You could have been killed!'

Tom forced a smile. 'No, no, seriously, it wasn't that big a deal. We're fine now, aren't we Lloyd?'

'Yes, Tom, we're fine.'

'Well, all right,' said Lou. 'But I've a mind to complain to the cab company.'

'Oh, you don't want to be bothered with that,' said Tom. 'You've got all those revisions to make.'

'Yes,' said Lloyd. 'You have to rewrite *Treasure Island*.' He stepped past Lou and clambered up into the cab.

Lou gazed at Tom suspiciously. '*Treasure Island*?' he murmured.

Lloyd's voice came from within the cab. 'I've decided, Papa, that *is* the better title. Tom convinced me.'

Tom shrugged his shoulders. 'Go figure,' he said and he too, climbed up into the cab.

Lou stood for a moment, thinking about it. Then, with a shake of his head, he signalled to the driver that he should turn the vehicle around. He climbed up into the cab, pulling the door shut behind him and the three of them went on their way.

Ten

Tom tried to sleep but it wasn't easy. Frances had lit the fire in the guest room to warm the place up and the dull glow of the coals illuminated the room with an eerie red glow. She had also found him an old-fashioned nightshirt to wear – one of Lloyd's, so it fit Tom's chunkier frame a little too snugly – and he tossed and turned for several hours while a succession of thoughts and images passed through his mind. He didn't like the fact that Lloyd now knew so much about him and he didn't really trust the boy to keep the information to himself.

Furthermore, the knowledge that William McSweeny had somehow survived being dunked in a barrel of quicklime and was still hell-bent on revenge, tormented him, because who knew when and where he might turn up next?

He was dimly aware of a distant church bell tolling three o'clock when he finally began to drift off. Even as he descended into the warm arms of sleep, he was aware of the stirring of black and white feathers in the air above him and he found himself wondering what a magpie had to do with all this. But then he was sinking like a stone into the depths, leaving not a ripple behind him.

*

'Tom, wake up!'

He blinked himself awake and registered that sunlight was spilling through the window of his bedroom. Almost as quickly, he realised that he was in a different room to the one he had fallen asleep in. He was back in his bedroom in Fairmilehead and it was Mum who was standing beside his bed, smiling fondly down at him. He was relieved to see that there were no bruises on her face.

'Come on, sleepyhead, it's nearly ten o'clock. Get dressed and get yourself down for breakfast. Hamish is waiting for you.'

He got himself into a sitting position and looked at her warily. 'Hamish?' he muttered.

'Yes. Did you forget? You're going to the Writers' Museum today.'

'Er . . . no, of course not.' He glanced around the room, checking for any differences, but everything looked reassuringly familiar – his clothes draped messily across a chair, his iPod and Kindle sitting on the bedside cabinet, his computer on the small writing desk. But still he was wary. He knew only too well how the supposedly normal could turn out to be anything but. Mum was already heading for the door.

'Breakfast will be on the table in ten minutes,' she

told him. 'Be there.' She went out, closing the door behind her.

Tom sighed, shook the last traces of sleep from his head and threw back the covers. He was glad to see that he was no longer wearing a long cotton nightshirt but a pair of striped pyjamas. He went out to the bathroom and performed his morning ritual. The face that looked back at him from the mirror was definitely his (there'd been one terrifying occasion when it had belonged to somebody else) so he brushed his teeth and headed back to his room, noting as he did so the appetising aroma of bacon wafting from downstairs. He dressed himself (his normal clothes, good,) and took a moment to switch on the Kindle. He found that he was still halfway through *Treasure Island*, exactly where he'd left off reading it. On an impulse he scrolled back to the title page just to check that it wasn't called *The Sea Cook*, but no, that too was still the same. On the next page, there was the photograph of Lou, exactly as Tom remembered him and on the next page—

'Oh. My. God,' whispered Tom. There was the book's dedication, which he knew had previously been to S.L.O, Samuel Lloyd Osbourne. But now, it read slightly differently.

To Tom Afflick, an English gentleman in accordance with whose classic taste the following narrative has been designed, it is now, in return for numerous delightful hours, and with the kindest wishes, dedicated by his affectionate friend, the author.

He stared at the dedication, as if he hoped that doing so might change it back to its original form. But annoyingly it stayed exactly the same as it was. What was he supposed to do about *this*? How was he ever going to explain it if anybody noticed – and it *would* be noticed, it was only a matter of time before somebody did and started asking awkward questions. Like, who was this mysterious friend of Robert Louis Stevenson and why didn't he feature in any history books?

'Tom? Breakfast!'

'Er, coming!' Tom switched the Kindle off and hurried downstairs to the kitchen. Hamish was already sitting at the table, applying lashings of ketchup to a plate of bacon and eggs. He winked at Tom.

'Morning, Tom,' he said, all jovial and friendly. 'Did you sleep all right?'

Tom nodded. He was trying to think what to do for the best. Obviously, everything depended on him getting back to 1881, but he had no control over *that*, he could only hope that it would happen sooner or later, and if and when it *did* happen his priority would be to make sure that the dedication got switched back to Lloyd. Otherwise, who knew what might come of it?

'I'm breaking the diet for once,' Hamish informed him, cheerfully. 'As it's a special day.'

Tom regarded him suspiciously. 'What's so special about it?' he asked.

'We're having a lad's day out,' said Hamish.

Mum brought over two more plates of food and

placed one in front of Tom. He gave her a pleading look. 'You're not coming with us?' he muttered.

'*I'm* going shopping,' she told him brightly. 'With a couple of my girlfriends. You boys can spend as long as you like finding out about . . . what's-his-name again?'

'Robert Louis Stevenson,' said Hamish. 'The Governor. You know, I've always meant to visit the Writers' Museum. Now I've finally got an excuse.' He picked up a sheaf of papers from beside his plate and handed them to Tom.

'Thought we might make a bit of a project of it,' he said. 'Printed that little lot off Wikipedia.' He filled his mouth with bacon and chewed noisily. 'Come on, eat up, I'm raring to go.'

Tom started eating, but with rather less enthusiasm. 'You know,' he said, 'you don't have to come with me. I mean, if you've got something better to do . . .'

'You are joking, I hope? I've been looking forward to this. Even took a day off work for it.'

Mum beamed lovingly at Hamish across the table. 'Perhaps you'd rather come shopping with me and the girls,' she suggested and they both laughed at the notion.

'It'll be great,' Hamish assured Tom. 'We'll have a good long look around the museum and then we'll pick up a spot of lunch somewhere. I thought we might go to Howie's and have something really traditional . . .'

He rattled on, but Tom wasn't listening. He was desperately hoping there weren't going to be any surprises in store at the museum.

They went into town on the bus because Hamish didn't want to be bothered finding a place to park. He was charm itself on the way in, pointing out places of interest to Tom, telling him how such and such a café was where he met his first girlfriend and how this club used to have the best music in Edinburgh and that tavern was where he'd drunk his first legal pint. Tom just nodded and grunted every so often because he had a lot on his mind. He was trying to decide if he'd come back to reality or one of the alternate worlds he'd sometimes encountered. So far, everything seemed normal enough, if you discounted how downright chummy Hamish was being.

After a short walk through the city centre, they found themselves on the Lawnmarket. Tom had good reason to remember *this* place. After all, it was where the murderer, William Burke had been hanged in January 1829 and though Tom had actually left before the execution, everyone at Tanner's Close had been talking about nothing else in the weeks before it happened.

The approach to the museum was in a little courtyard and Tom noticed that special flagstones had been installed around the place with quotes from famous writers. After a little searching they found Lou's.

There are no stars so lovely
as Edinburgh street-lamps.

'Isn't that just fantastic?' enthused Hamish, and Tom decided that the man was trying a little bit too hard now. Hamish pointed to the museum itself, a lofty grey stone building with a turret-like entrance. 'Now,' he said, 'I did a wee bit of research on the internet. There are basically three writers represented here. Sir Walter Scott, Robert Burns and Robert Louis Stevenson. I suggest we concentrate on RLS today, and if you've a mind to consider the other two, we can always come again.'

'Whatever,' said Tom. He was starting to feel rather weary of Hamish's constant cheerfulness.

'Right then, step this way.' Hamish led him in through the open door and, following the signs, they went down a narrow flight of circular stone steps to the basement room. It was a large rectangular space with deep red walls. These were hung with paintings and black and white photographs. In various glass cases around the room were artefacts that had belonged to the great author himself. There was nobody else down there, so they were at liberty to wander about and have a good look.

They stopped in front of a large colour painting of Lou which depicted him standing by an open doorway in a strangely exaggerated pose, one hand lifted to his mouth, the other in his pocket. Sitting on a sofa to the right of him was Frances who, for reasons best known to herself, was draped in an oriental-style robe of white and gold. A caption beneath the painting said that it was by John Singer Sargent.

'That's when you know you've arrived,' said

Hamish. 'When a famous painter wants to do your portrait.'

Tom nodded, but he thought it was a poor likeness that did neither Lou nor Fran any favours at all. Hamish moved on to the next image, a large black and white photograph, while Tom lingered by the painting, seeing if he could recognise the view through the open doorway, which showed a gloomy staircase leading upwards. It definitely wasn't the hired rooms where the Stevensons had spent Christmas 1881, he decided. The family house in Heriot Place perhaps?

'Ah,' said Hamish. 'I read about this.'

Tom moved across to join him and looked at the picture. It showed the Stevenson family and a whole bunch of other people, sitting on the veranda of a house in a tropical setting. Tom's gaze flicked down to the caption, which read, 'On the veranda of Valima, Samoa, 1892.' He looked back at the picture. There was Lou, dressed in khaki shirt and trousers and the tall youth lounging beside him, also dressed in khakis and wearing some kind of pith helmet, was undoubtedly Lloyd, but much taller and older than when Tom had last seen him. Fran was sitting beside Lou, her Victorian-style dress looking highly inappropriate for such a climate and lounging at her feet was a young woman with dark hair. Tom supposed this must be Belle, the stepdaughter, who Lloyd had told him was married and lived elsewhere. Also in the picture were various natives, bare-chested and wearing patterned sarongs.

'This is where Stevenson finished up his life,' said Hamish, pulling the Wikipedia pages out of the pocket of his overcoat. He consulted it for a moment. 'Yeah, he was dead two years after this picture was taken. At the age of forty-four.' He shook his head. 'That's no age at all, really.'

Tom felt as though he'd just been punched in the chest. It hadn't occurred to him that the Robert Louis Stevenson he'd met in 1881 had only eleven years left to live.

'Where's Samoa?' asked Tom.

'In the South Pacific, I think.'

'I suppose he'd gone there because of the tuberculosis,' murmured Tom. 'Is that what killed him in the end?'

'Oh, no, he died of a . . .' Hamish checked the facts. 'A cerebral haemorrhage. It happened while he was making mayonnaise, of all things! And anyway, they don't think it *was* tuberculosis.'

Tom looked at him. 'What do you mean?'

'It's here somewhere . . .' Hamish scanned the pages for a moment. 'Where did I see it? Ah yes, here it is. They think it was most probably something called sarcoidosis.'

'I never heard of that,' said Tom.

'I don't think anybody knew about it until recently,' said Hamish. 'Shame. Just think how many more great books he could have written if he'd only had more time.' He handed the pages over to Tom. 'Here, you should read these when you get the chance.'

'Thanks.' Tom folded the sheets and stuffed them into the pocket of his overcoat, telling himself he'd give them a proper look when he had a bit more time.

Hamish moved on to the next photograph, but Tom lingered for a moment, staring back at the author's face. Lou looked serene in the picture, contented. He could have had no idea that his time was already running out.

Beside him he heard Hamish say, 'Jesus!'

He turned and looked at his stepfather in surprise. 'Are you all right?' he asked. Hamish was staring open-mouthed at the next photograph in the line. His hands hung limply by his sides and he seemed to be having trouble breathing. Tom moved across to see what Hamish was staring at.

Now it was Tom's turn to take a deep breath, because staring back at him, across an interval of hundreds of years, was his own face.

'That's *you*,' hissed Hamish.

'It looks a bit like me,' admitted Tom. 'But . . .'

He knew it was pointless to protest, because the figure was also wearing the same clothes that Tom was wearing now – jeans, trainers and the t-shirt featuring the gorilla in a top hat. He was standing beside a grinning Lou, a smiling Fran and a scowling Lloyd, who was dressed in that hideous sailor suit he always wore. The four of them were posed beside a little Christmas tree and the caption read, *Christmas 1881, Edinburgh.*

'You, you knew Robert Louis Stevenson,' said Hamish. 'You *met* him. Why didn't you tell me?'

'I . . . don't be daft, how could I have met him? That's, that's been photoshopped.' He pointed to the caption. 'Look, that was taken in 1881. How could I possibly have . . .?'

But Hamish wasn't listening. He was breathing heavily now, his shoulders rising and falling and Tom couldn't help but notice how the fabric of his winter coat appeared to be stretching across his already brawny shoulders, as though he was growing bigger, broader, even more muscular. As Tom stared in dumbstruck horror, he saw that tufts of thick red hair were sprouting from the back of Hamish's neck.

'Hamish, are you−?'

He broke off as Hamish turned to glare at him and now the man's face was changing, even as Tom stared at it, mesmerised. It was stretching, reshaping itself like warm clay, the forehead elongating, the cheeks sprouting clumps of luxurious auburn hair, the eyes turning a vivid shade of amber. When he spoke again, his voice was guttural, beastlike. Large discoloured teeth jutted down over his bottom lip.

'You should have told me!' he bellowed and his voice seemed to fill the entire room. 'You should have said.' He pointed a big, hairy finger at Tom and the nail of that finger was yellow and misshapen. He began to advance threateningly and Tom backed away in alarm.

'Hamish,' he whispered. 'T . . . take it easy.'

'You let me bring you here under false pretences,' snarled Hamish. 'You wanted to make a fool of me!'

'No, no, I . . .' Tom broke off as Hamish launched a savage punch at his face. He ducked to one side and Hamish's fist sped past and connected with a glass cabinet, smashing it to pieces. Tom stared down at it in dismay. 'Whoah, stop! This stuff is valuable. You can't . . .'

Hamish threw an arm around Tom's neck and pulled him in close, almost stifling him with the powerful animal-like stench that was emanating from him.

'You're making me angry!' he bellowed and with that, he picked Tom up as though he weighed no more than a bundle of clothing and threw him clear across the room. Tom collided with a large painting and brought it crashing to the ground, tearing the canvas and splintering the ornate frame. He groaned, rolled over amidst the debris and scrambled to his feet, only to see that Hamish had now become a total changeling. His heavy coat had torn across his shoulders, exposing a great hairy back.

Mr Hyde. The two words flashed through Tom's mind as Hamish clambered up onto an antique writing desk and prepared to launch himself across the room. Tom didn't feel inclined to wait around and see what happened next. He turned and ran for the exit, aware of a crashing sound behind him and the thud of heavy feet on the carpeted floor. He made it as far as the spiral staircase and started up them, but he'd only taken half a dozen steps when a great hairy hand clamped around his ankle and pulled back hard, wrenching him off his feet. He fell and his forehead connected with the stone step, sending a shock of liquid pain pulsing through him. Coloured lights exploded in front of his eyes, the world began to see-saw madly around him and he was only dimly aware that something was pulling him backwards. He flipped himself around and saw Mr Hyde, crouched over him. He was chuckling fiendishly, ready to finish Tom off . . .

And then mercifully, the darkness closed around him, like a warm enveloping cloak and he knew no more.

Eleven

When he finally came to, he was lying in bed at the
Stevenson's house and the light of early morning was
leaking through a gap in the curtains. He could hear
the sound of a horse's hooves clopping along the street
outside. He felt absolutely exhausted but not in any
pain, which was a mercy, and when he lifted a hand
to prod gingerly at his forehead, everything there felt
fine. He pushed aside the sheets to find that he was once
again wearing Lloyd's long cotton nightgown. He got
out of bed and stumbled across to a small mirror on the
far wall, but when he studied his reflection he found no
sign of any injury to his head and was left to wonder,
once again, if what had happened to him had been
merely a dream or an alternate reality. Since there were
no bruises in evidence, he suspected the former, but he
had long ago given up trying to figure out the difference
between the two. Sometimes he wondered if there
was a difference.

He heard sounds of movement coming from below
so he changed into his clothes and went down to

find Fran in her customary place at the kitchen table, drinking tea. Anna was busy at the cooking range but there was no sign of Lou or Lloyd, this morning.

'Ah, Tom,' said Fran. 'I'm glad you're up. I wanted a word with you.'

Tom took a seat beside her. 'Where are the others?' he asked.

Fran looked grave. 'Lloyd's with Lou,' she said. 'Lou was awake all night with that darned cough. I'm starting to think that if he's to have any respite from it, we really should head back to Davos, with all speed. But he's as stubborn as ever. He's insisting that we stay on, at least until after Hogmanay.' She shook her head, frowned. 'Tom, I wanted to speak to you about this business with Miss McCallum. Clearly you haven't been exactly truthful with us.'

'Oh, that, well . . .'

'I don't really understand why you'd tell us you were staying with her when she is out of the country.'

'Erm, it's kind of . . .' Tom thought for a moment. 'I explained all this to Lou, last night. Didn't he tell you about me running away from home?'

'Yes, he *did* tell me, but that's hardly an explanation. Lou also suggested that I should get the address of your parents and write them a letter, explaining where you are.'

'There's no point in doing that,' said Tom. 'They wouldn't get the letter.'

'Why not?'

'Because . . . because they aren't there now. I told you, they're in the South of France.'

'So that bit at least is true?'

Tom nodded. 'Yeah, like I said, they wanted to be on their own for a bit. And you see, I don't have their address over there.'

'Which means they left you completely on your own. A boy of fourteen? Perhaps it's the police I should be contacting?'

'Oh, er, no, don't do that! Cat will explain everything when she gets back.'

'Cat?' Fran raised her eyebrows.

'I mean Miss McCallum! It's sort of my nickname for her,' he explained. 'It's what I used to call her when she was, when she was . . .' He broke off awkwardly. He'd been about to say, 'When she was my age,' but realised that that wouldn't help matters at all, 'when we first met,' he ended lamely.

'And how long ago was that? With respect, Tom, you're only a boy and she's quite elderly. And I don't mind telling you, I really don't think it's respectful referring to her as "Cat".'

'She doesn't mind. She *likes* that name.' Tom sighed. 'Look, I really *do* know her,' he said. 'If you're thinking that I made it all up, I . . .'

'Oh, I don't doubt for a moment that you *know* her. And, yes, for your information, Miss McCallum is back in residence. Apparently, she arrived late last night. Her manservant must have told her all about our attempts to contact her, because a messenger arrived with a note from her this morning.'

'Oh really? What did she say?'

'The note wasn't for me,' Fran assured him. She

picked up a cream coloured envelope from the table and handed it to Tom. On it was written, in an ornate hand, just two words: Tom Afflick.

He gazed at it for a moment, then tore it open and scanned the single sheet of paper within.

Tom

Can it really be true? Have you actually returned?
Or is it just the sick fancy of a demented old woman?
If it really is you, please, visit me with all haste.
I curse the fact that I was away in England if it
means that I have missed the event I have waited
a lifetime for. Please, do not hesitate. I shall have
no thought of rest until I have seen you again.

Cat

Tom folded the letter. He looked up at Fran who had been studying him intently as he read it. 'I need to go and see her,' he said.

Fran nodded. 'Of course. You'll have some breakfast before you leave?'

'Umm, no, that's all right, thanks. It sounds like she's pretty anxious to see me.' He started to get up from the table, but Fran put a hand on his arm to keep him in place for a moment.

'I hope we will see more of you before we go back to Davos,' she said. 'I'm sure I don't have to tell you that Lou is very fond of you, as indeed, we all are.

I think Lou regards you as some kind of . . . muse. You've certainly fired him up with regard to *Treasure Island*. He's already begun on those revisions, you know. I told him he should rest for a while, but he's having none of it. He's sitting up in bed, editing page after page. It's as though he's on a mission.'

Tom smiled. 'It'll be worth it,' he said. He looked at Fran. 'Did it ever occur to you,' he said, 'that maybe it isn't tuberculosis that Lou has?'

She frowned. 'What else could it be?' she asked him.

He thought about telling her that it was actually sarcoidosis but quickly realised that there would be no point. The illness wouldn't be identified for another hundred years or more. 'I don't know,' he said, flatly. 'Just . . . something they don't have a name for yet?'

Fran shrugged her shoulders. 'How I only wish there was a cure for whatever it is,' she said. 'It is the curse of his life at the moment. And I sometimes fear that it will not be a long one.' She made an attempt to brighten up and forced a smile. 'Anyhow, please look in on him and say goodbye before you leave,' she begged him. 'And listen, we're having a little get-together this evening for Christmas Eve and all. William will be there and a few other of Lou's friends. If you'd like to come, we'd be absolutely delighted to see you. And Miss McCallum too, of course, if she's up to visiting.'

'Okay, I'll mention it to her,' said Tom. 'Thanks for everything.' He stood up and was about to reach out and shake her hand, but on second thoughts, he leaned forward and planted a polite peck on her cheek. She gave him an odd look and then smiled. 'You Manchester people are so forward,' she said, but he could see that she was actually rather delighted by the informality of his action.

'That's us,' admitted Tom, as he headed out of the room. 'Oh, yeah, we're famous for it.'

*

Up on the first floor he found Lou in his room, sitting in a big double bed. He was propped up on mounds of feather pillows with a blanket draped around his shoulders and was scribbling furiously away on a sheet of manuscript paper with a simple metal dip pen. The pages rested on an ingenious wooden writing box which sat on the bed in front of him. Lloyd was lounging on the carpet next to the bed, playing with some brightly painted lead soldiers. Both Lou and Lloyd looked up as Tom stepped into the room.

'Ah, there you are!' Lou looked pale and washed-out, Tom thought, and he noticed that his free hand held a bundled up handkerchief that was liberally spotted with dried blood. An idea occurred to Tom. What if, on one of his trips back to the present-day, he could go to a doctor and pick up a prescription? Something that would actually help the symptoms of sarcoidosis. If indeed, there *was* such a thing. But, he thought, how would he ever convince a doctor to give him the medicine? It wasn't as though he could fake the symptoms. He remembered the miracles his pack of antibiotics had effected in 1645, how he had managed to cure two cases of bubonic plague with them. But in that instance, he'd actually had the pills in his pocket when he'd first travelled back.

'As you can see, I'm already working on the rewrite,' said Lou, interrupting his thoughts.

'Huh? Oh yeah, good for you,' said Tom. 'I just popped up to say that I'm heading over to see Cat, I mean, Miss McCallum.'

'Yes, Fran said she'd sent you a note. But please tell us we haven't seen the last of you.' He glanced at Lloyd. 'We like having Tom around, don't we, Lloyd?'

'Oh, yeah, he's a tonic.' Lloyd was studying Tom with a knowing smirk on his face and Tom remembered that the boy now knew everything about him. 'You be careful out there, Tom,' he said. 'We don't want you coming to any harm.'

'No, I'll er . . . watch out,' said Tom. 'Thanks.'

'Did Fran mention the party tonight?' asked Lou.

Tom nodded. 'She did.'

'See if you can get Catriona to come along,' Lou urged him. 'She's fine company when a fellow can coax her out, but she so rarely goes anywhere these days. I'm sure she'd enjoy the company of some other writers. And you know, there's many of us in the literary world who feel that *The Path of Truth* is one of *the* great novels.'

'Yeah, it's a top book, isn't it?'

Lou looked surprised. 'You've read it?' he cried.

'Yeah, 'course I have. I'll tell her you said that, if you like.'

'By all means.' Lou shook his head. 'I must say Tom, you're full of surprises. Anyway, I'm sure you're looking forward to seeing her again.'

'I expect Tom and Miss McCallum have a lot to talk about,' said Lloyd, slyly. 'Maybe they want to discuss the good old days.'

Lou looked from Tom to Lloyd and back again. 'Am I missing something here?' he asked.

'No, nothing!' said Tom, a little too loudly. He pointed to the sheets of paper beside the writing box. 'You just crack on with that. I'm really looking forward to finding out what happens in the stockade.'

As soon as he'd said it, he knew he'd made a mistake.

'The stockade?' echoed Lou. He was staring intently at Tom.

'Er, yeah, that's where I got to on the train. You know, the bit where Jim and Squire Trelawney and the others, they go in the old stockade and the . . . the pirates have got them surrounded, so . . .'

'But that chapter hasn't appeared in *Young Folks* yet,' protested Lou.

'Oh, I . . . I'm sure it has.'

Lou shook his head. 'That's still another two editions away.' Lou looked suddenly rather stern. 'Perhaps you'd like to explain, Tom, how you know all about a scene that has yet to appear in print?'

There was a terrible silence, while Tom tried desperately to come up with a convincing answer. 'Well, I, I . . .' His mind was a blank.

But then Lloyd said, 'I told him about it, Papa.'

Tom stared at Lloyd in amazement. 'Oh, er . . . yeah, that's right! We were talking about it, weren't we Lloyd? I was wondering what happened next, and you – you sort of told me and . . . then I must have thought I'd read it for myself.' He slapped his forehead. 'What am I like?' he said. 'Duh!'

'I see.' Lou seemed to accept the explanation, but he gave Lloyd an admonishing look. 'I'm surprised at you,' he said. 'What have I told you about giving the story away? Always let the reader . . .'

'Discover it for himself,' finished Lloyd. 'Yes, sorry Papa. I guess I wasn't thinking.'

Lou gestured to the half-written sheet. 'Well, I'd better get back to it. I hope we'll see you tonight, Tom. And if not tonight then definitely before we head back to Davos.'

'Sure, no worries.' Tom glanced at Lloyd and saw that the boy was studying him, a superior smirk on his face. Lloyd had got him out of a sticky situation all right, but Tom wasn't stupid enough to think that the boy had done it out of the goodness of his heart. There'd be an ulterior motive waiting to be revealed somewhere further down the line, of that Tom was sure.

'Well, catch you guys later!' he said and turning away, he headed along the landing and down the stairs. He needed to visit Cat and he sincerely hoped that this time nothing would happen to prevent the reunion. He grabbed his coat from the stand in the hall on his way through and opened the door. Outside, the Edinburgh day looked perfectly normal. He stood for a moment and then went down the steps, one at a time, placing his feet with great care, terrified that the stones would turn to liquid beneath them and pull him in. But this time they stayed reassuringly solid.

He made it down to the pavement and hesitated, looking suspiciously around. Strangers moved to and fro along the street but for the moment at least, there was no sign of a mysterious cloaked figure.

'So far, so good,' he muttered and began to walk.

Twelve

Cat's house in Lauriston Street was a grand affair, a lofty, grey stone mansion in the heart of the old town. Tom climbed the steps to the door and rang the bell. Now that the moment was close at hand, he felt strangely anxious. After all, the last time he'd seen her she'd been his age. Now she was an old woman. However things turned out, it was going to feel very weird.

The door opened and a man in a tail coat and striped trousers stood there, gazing down at Tom with a grim expression on his face, as though he didn't much like what he saw. 'May I help you?' he said, flatly.

'Er, I'm here to see Cat . . . Catriona. I mean, Miss McCallum! My name is Tom Afflick.'

The reaction was dramatic. The man swung the door wide and ushered Tom inside. 'If you'd be so good as to follow me, sir,' he said. 'I shall take you directly to her.' He waited till Tom was inside then closed the door and led him along a hallway, a much wider, grander one than the Stevenson's hired place. Through open doorways to his left and right, Tom glimpsed massive rooms, richly furnished with gilt chairs and tables, the walls hung with huge oil paintings. Cut glass chandeliers hung from the ceilings, reflecting the light from massive windows. Finally, they came to a door at the very end of the hall. The man knocked politely then turned the handle in one white-gloved hand and, holding the door open, he stepped aside and bowed his head, waiting for Tom to enter. Tom did as he was bid, feeling faintly embarrassed by the man's politeness. He stepped into the room and the door closed behind him.

She was sitting in a chair reading a book, but she looked up in surprise as Tom entered and one hand flew to her mouth while the book slipped from her other hand and tumbled, forgotten, to the floor. She got to her feet then and Tom could see how much she had aged. Her hair, once long and blonde, was now as white as a fall of snow, tied back from her face, which was lined and creased by the passing years. But her eyes were just as he remembered them, keen and glittering with intelligence. Behind her, above a marble fireplace, hung her portrait, as she had looked in her fifties. Tom knew the picture well. The last time he'd seen it, it had been hanging in the National Museum of Scotland, above a glass case of Cat's possessions and a brief history listing the various novels she had published. One particular story, that had never seen publication, was an alleged early science fiction novel called *The Traveller In Time*. A book she'd dedicated to Tom.

There was a long silence while they stood looking at each other. Then Tom felt that somebody needed to speak. 'Hey, Cat,' he said, affecting the broad Mancunian accent that he knew she loved "Ow yer doin', chuck?'

Her eyes filled with tears. She hurried over to him and they embraced. In his arms her thin figure seemed to have no substance at all and she was trembling against him, as though trying to suppress powerful emotions.

'So it's true,' she whispered at last. 'I scarcely dared to hope, but it really *is* you. After all these years.' She stepped back from him and held him at arm's length. 'And you look exactly as I remember you,' she told him. 'Exactly.'

'Steady on,' he told her. 'I'm a whole year older than I was!'

She seemed to grow suddenly self-conscious and lifted her hands to cover her face. 'But what must you think of me?' she cried. 'What a horrible sight, I must be. Oh Tom, why did you have to wait so long?'

He took her hands in his and pulled them back down to her sides. 'I didn't have any say over it,' he assured her. 'I never do. It's just chance that brought me to this year. But I'm glad it did. I always hoped I'd see you again, one day.'

'But not like this,' she said and another tear trickled down her face.

'It doesn't matter,' he assured her. 'The main thing is, we're together again and that's really cool.' He gave her a warm smile. 'So, tell me, what's been happening? Did I miss much?'

She shook her head. 'Where would I start?' she asked him. 'So many years have flown . . . more than fifty of them.' She thought for a moment. 'I . . . I've published some books,' she said.

'I know. There's information about you in the National Museum of Scotland. Or at least, there *will* be.' He pointed to the picture above the fireplace. 'And that picture's there too. In the future, Cat, you're going to be a big name in feminism.'

'In what?' she murmured.

'Er . . .' He tried to think of a simpler way to put it. 'In, women's rights? You remember when we first met, how you used to say that women should have the same rights as men and how they should be treated as equals? Well, in the future, they *will* be and it's because of people like you that it happened . . . or *will* happen.'

She looked stunned. 'I'll be remembered?' she whispered. 'I never dared hope for that much. You know, I wrote a book about you, Tom. *The* . . .'

'. . . *Traveller In Time*. Yeah, I read about that in the museum. They reckoned you invented science fiction with that one.' He noticed her puzzled look and elaborated. 'That's going to be big too.'

'I'm not familiar with the term,' she told him. 'I believe the novels of Jules Verne have been described as scientific romances.'

'Yeah, well you got there before him, didn't you?'

'But my story isn't fiction. It's an account of what happened to me. To *us*.'

'Yeah, but people aren't going to know that, are they? They'll think you just made it up.'

There was a silence then, as they stood gazing at each other. Then Cat seemed to recover a little. 'Well, come and . . . come and sit down. And take off your coat if you're staying. I'll get you some tea. You *do* still drink tea, I suppose?' Tom nodded and she pulled him across the room to a sofa and motioned for him to be seated. He threw his overcoat across the back of it and sat down. Cat picked up a little brass bell from a table and rang it. Almost instantly, the manservant bustled in to the room. 'Yes, madam?' he asked impassively.

'Please bring us some tea, Angus,' she told him. She glanced at Tom. 'And scones?' He nodded eagerly. 'And fresh scones. The very best that Moira has.'

Angus bowed. 'Of course, madam,' he said and went out of the room, closing the door behind him. Tom couldn't help but chuckle. Catriona looked at him enquiringly. 'What's wrong?' she asked.

'You've come a long way from Tanner's Close,' he observed. 'You're obviously *minted*.'

She frowned, not recognising the term.

'I mean, dead rich!' He waved a hand at his lush surroundings. 'How did all this happen?'

She sighed, rolled her eyes then took a seat beside him. 'The only way that any woman of my class ever achieves such things,' she said. 'I was lucky in matrimony.'

'Huh?'

'I married a rich man. The owner of a flour mill.'

'You're married?' Tom looked nervously around, half-expecting to see a strange man lurking in the background.

'I *was* married. My husband, Josiah, died three

years ago.' She gave Tom a challenging look. 'Well, I couldn't wait around forever in the hope that you'd return, could I? And Josiah was a good man, a kind man.'

'And a rich man,' added Tom. 'Obvs.'

Cat looked worried at that. 'I don't want you to think that I'm some kind of gold-digger,' she said. 'He wasn't rich when I met him, but the wealth came as he developed his business. We were happy together, the two of us, but I couldn't give him children, which was a great regret to both of us. When he died there was nobody to inherit, so . . . all the money came to me. And when I am gone, it will go into a charitable trust I've established to help young women from poor backgrounds better themselves.'

'Wow, that's pretty cool,' said Tom. 'But something was puzzling him. 'So, if you were married . . .?'

'Yes?'

'How come you're still a McCallum?'

'Because I insisted on keeping the name,' she told him. 'I'd already published my first novel using it and, as I explained to Josiah, a woman is not a commodity to be purchased and adjusted according to the whims of a man. I told him if he wanted me, he must accept that notion. Happily, he agreed to it.'

'Hey, there's no messing with you, is there? I can see why your picture's in the National Museum.'

She waved a hand to dismiss the idea, as though it was of no great importance. 'But what of you, Tom? What's happened to you since you left me stranded on Arthur's Seat all those years ago?'

'Not much,' he assured her. 'Remember, it's only been a year for me. I've been at school, hanging with my mates. I've reached another level on *Grand Theft Auto*.' He smiled, as he realised how meaningless that must sound. He thought back to that day on the hill and remembered why they had gone there in the first place. 'One thing I don't understand,' he said. 'The coffins?'

'Ah, the coffins.' She nodded, smiled wistfully. 'There's been so much speculation about them over the years, hasn't there?'

'Yes, but when they were found, it must have been, what . . . only eight years later? You must have heard about it?'

'I could hardly miss it,' she said. 'It was in all the papers. People talked of witchcraft and sailors drowned at sea and all manner of strange things.'

'So, why didn't you tell people that *you'd* put them there? And why?'

Cat sighed. 'There didn't seem to be much point,' she said. 'My brother was dead by then and . . .'

'Fraser?' Tom stared at her. 'Oh, no, Cat. What happened to him?'

'War happened to him,' she said. 'Oh, you remember what he was like, Tom, with his toy soldiers and his military books. He enlisted in the British Army at his first opportunity and ended up as an officer, dying in some obscure war in the Cape of Africa, a place I cannot even pronounce.' She stared at her hands for a moment. 'Such a waste. Yet, somehow, also an inevitability. He was the one who made the coffins, of course, with a little help from the two of us. When I heard that they'd been found, I thought to myself, well, there's too much in this world that is explained. Why not leave a little mystery for people to ponder? I've always been rather fond of a good mystery.'

She looked at Tom. 'I suppose I could have told everyone the truth. That I left them there as a tribute to Jamie Wilson and the other victims of Burke and Hare, when I was a girl of fourteen, aided by a boy who had travelled back in time. Oh, I'm sure they'd all have been perfectly happy to accept *that* story.' She chuckled and the years seemed to slip away from her. He could see once again the mischievous girl he had first met back in 1828. 'I suppose I could leave a letter to be opened after my death, explaining everything, but even that idea seems somehow unnecessary.' Her eyes narrowed. 'What of that, Tom? In that museum of yours, I suppose it must have registered the year of my death?'

'I suppose so. I really don't remember,' he said and was shocked to realise that this was true. He *must* have seen the year of her death, in passing, but it hadn't really registered with him at the time. And now he was glad that he couldn't recall it.

'Well, whatever it was, I don't imagine I have all that long left. These days I feel my age in every bone.' She looked at Tom sadly. 'And here's you, so young, so full of life, as though the passing of time means nothing.'

She seemed to sense his discomfort and made an attempt to change the subject. 'So, have you an idea what *did* bring you back to this particular year?'

He nodded. 'Robert Louis Stevenson,' he said. 'I think you know him. I was reading one of his books just before it happened. Oh, not one that's been published yet – something that will be out in a year or so. Cat, he's going to be *huge*.'

She looked puzzled. 'He's such a slim young fellow,' she said.

'No, I mean he's going to be very famous. Even in my time, people will be reading his stuff.'

'Yes, well of course I *did* realise that you were staying with the Stevensons. And I *have* met him on several occasions. He seems an extraordinarily talented young man . . .'

'Oh, you don't know the half of it. Cat, he's going to be bigger than J. K. Rowling.'

'Who?' she muttered.

'Bigger than–' He tried to think of an example of a writer who would mean something to her, but couldn't think of one. Then a thought occurred to him. He reached into the pocket of his overcoat which was still draped over the back of the sofa and sure enough, there were the rolled sheets of paper that Hamish had given him in the Writers' Museum. Which made him realise that it couldn't all have been a dream, otherwise he wouldn't have these printouts in his pocket. He unfolded the pages. 'Here, let me show you these,' he said. 'It's hard to explain exactly what they are, but in the future . . .'

He broke off, puzzled, as he realised that most of the pages were blank. He saw that the Wikipedia entry, which had previously run to something like nine pages, now only extended to two. Tom scanned them in dismay. Apart from the few short stories and essays that Lou had already published by 1881, there was only one other publication mentioned, the serialisation of *Treasure Island: or The Wreck of the Hispaniola* in *Young Folks* magazine, under the name Captain George North.

'Oh, no,' he murmured.

Cat gave him a look of concern. 'Is something wrong?' she asked him.

'It's just, according to this, Lou isn't famous any more. Or at least, he isn't *going* to be if I don't make some changes at this end.'

She gave him a shrewd look. 'Are you tinkering with time again?' she asked him.

'Not exactly. But, I think I might already have changed it a bit, accidentally.' He pondered for a moment. 'Well, don't worry, it ain't over till the fat lady sings.'

'I beg your pardon?'

'Never mind.' Tom stuffed the sheets of paper back into the pocket of his coat and told himself he'd apply himself to this new problem just as soon as he got an opportunity. For the moment, there were other things to talk about. 'Before I forget, Cat, the Stevensons are having a little get-together this evening at their house and we're both invited.'

Cat looked doubtful. 'Oh, I don't know,' she said. 'I don't get out much these days. Nobody wants a lonely old woman making everybody melancholy.'

'Well, you won't be lonely tonight, will you?' he

assured her. 'I'll be your date. And Lou was telling me that he really rates your writing.'

She looked doubtful. 'He said that?'

'Yeah, absolutely. He thinks you're brilliant. There's going to be other writers there too. William Whats-His-Face, the one-legged poet?'

'Mr Henley?' she ventured.

'Yeah, that's him. Bearded guy, looks like a pirate. And maybe even the bloke who's going to write *Peter Pan*, but hasn't quite got around to it yet. And . . . oh, loads of others.' He looked at her. 'You will come, won't you?'

There was a polite tap at the door and Angus entered, carrying a silver platter heaped with tea things. He set them down on a low table in front of the sofa and Tom was delighted to see a plate piled high with fresh cream scones.

'Shall I pour the tea, madam?' asked Angus.

'No, no, we'll see to ourselves,' she told him. 'And tell Cook there'll be a guest for dinner this evening.' She looked at Tom. 'If you can stay that long,' she said.

'I'll try,' he told her and slipped her a wink.

Angus bowed and went out again, closing the door behind him.

'Hey, this is a bit of all right,' said Tom. He picked up the silver teapot. 'Shall I be Mother?' he asked, with a wink.

She laughed. 'Oh, you and your Manchester expressions!' she exclaimed. 'I noted them all down in my journals, you know. And I put some into *The Traveller In Time.*'

He poured tea. 'Yeah, so I believe. In the museum, it said something about your language being "experimental" for the time.' They both chuckled at that. 'I wish I could have read the one about me. But you never published it, did you?'

'No. I thought it would have raised too many difficult questions. And I was still a young girl when I wrote that one. It was quite . . . immature.'

'I read another of yours, though,' he told her. '*The Path of Truth*?' This was true, though he'd had the devil of a job getting hold of it. In the end, he'd managed to find it online through *Project Gutenberg* and had read the whole thing on his computer. It had taken him weeks to get through it.

'You've read *that*?' she murmured. 'Goodness knows what you must have made of it.'

It was true, it had been a struggle and his mates at school had wondered why he was reading some out-dated melodrama about a young woman, attempting to make her way in Victorian society, but he'd stuck with it, mostly because every other page or so there'd been something that reminded him of the young girl he'd known. 'I thought it was sick,' he told her. Then added, 'That means good, by the way.'

'I'm glad to hear it,' she said. 'But I suspect you're being kind. That's not a book intended for a young boy, particularly one from the twenty-first century.'

'I read it just the same. And I'm not the only one who thinks it rocks. Lou, that's Mr Stevenson, he told me it was one of the "great novels". Seriously, he thinks you're the dog's . . . he thinks you're like, a genius.' Cat watched as he stirred two big spoonfuls of sugar into his tea. 'Try a scone,' she suggested. 'Moira's very good in the kitchen but I'm afraid I'm a poor subject for her talents.'

He helped himself and took a huge bite. 'Umm, good,' he said, through a mouthful of food and Cat smiled fondly.

'Ah, I remember the days when I could eat like that,' she said. She, too, picked up a scone, and took a tiny nibble from the edge of it. 'I so wish my mother could have been alive to see my changing fortunes. She would have loved these scones. She was a fair baker herself, but we could never afford the fresh cream.'

'Mary?' Tom put his plate down for a moment. 'What happened to her?'

'She died perhaps five years after you left. She took a fever one summer and there was nothing we could do for her. It broke my poor father's heart. Oh, he carried on long enough to see me married, but he didn't dally for long after that. I always think that losing my mother took much of his heart away. He never had an interest in any other woman after her death.' She sighed. 'Listen to me,' she muttered. 'I'm like a prophet of doom! Little wonder nobody wants to share my company! Here, Tom, eat up.' She picked up his plate and thrust it back into his hands. 'Enough of the sad recollections, we should be looking to the future. Where I've no doubt you'll be returning, all too soon. Have you any idea how long you'll be staying this time?'

He shook his head. 'I really don't know. And Cat,

do you remember the last time I was here, I told you that there was someone . . . some*thing* chasing me?'

She nodded. 'I do remember, though I never saw him.'

'Well, he hasn't given up yet. I've seen him a couple of times already and I get the feeling he's kind of . . . homing in on me.'

Cat looked perturbed. 'Then we must do something about it,' she urged him. 'Should we call upon the services of the constabulary?'

He shook his head. 'I don't think there's much the cops can do about McSweeny. When I first came back in time, he was just a man. Now he's . . . something else.' He frowned. 'But don't worry, he hasn't caught up with me yet.'

He took another bite of his scone. 'This is delicious,' he said. 'Your Moira would go down a storm on the *Bake-Off*'

'The what?'

'Sorry, it's just this thing my mum likes to watch.'

They spent the afternoon in happy conversation and then ate dinner together, a sumptuous meal of several courses, served on silver plates in a huge dining room beneath a massive oil painting of a man dressed in a tail coat and an embroidered waistcoat. He was posed in front of a huge brick building with a sign above the door: *Josiah Finley, Flour Merchant*. He looked a decent enough bloke, Tom thought, even though he seemed to have lost most of his hair by the time the picture was painted.

'I wonder what Josiah would have thought?' murmured Cat. 'If I'd ever told him about you.'

'He'd have probably thought you'd been on the bottle,' said Tom and they both laughed.

'You know,' she said, 'I haven't enjoyed myself so much in years. I think I *will* come with you to that party.'

When the last course had been eaten Cat excused herself and went upstairs to prepare herself for the night out, leaving Tom to ponder his latest predicament. So, one moment *Treasure Island* was dedicated to him, the next, the book wasn't going to be written at all. So what had changed? And more importantly, what was Tom going to do about it?

He decided that he was going to go to the party with one aim in mind: to ensure Lou got back to work as soon as possible. And Catriona was going to have to help him.

Thirteen

When Tom and Cat arrived at the party, everything was in full swing; or, at least, in what Tom assumed passed for full swing in 1881. A maid politely took their coats and a manservant, who Tom assumed must have been specially hired for the occasion, escorted them to the front room, which was packed with little huddles of people, sipping glasses of sherry and talking earnestly with each other. Lou spotted the new arrivals straight away and hurried over to greet them, only to be joined a moment later by Fran.

'Ah, Tom, you made it,' said Lou. 'Excellent. And you persuaded Mrs McCallum to come also.' Lou reached out, took Cat's hand and politely kissed the back of it. 'I'm so pleased you decided to grace us with your presence. This is a true honour.'

'Somebody managed to talk me round,' said Cat, giving Tom a sidelong look. 'I confess I'm not a great party-goer these days.'

'So, how exactly do you two come to know each other?' asked Fran. 'We did ask Tom earlier but we didn't get an awful lot of sense out of him.'

Tom and Cat had anticipated this possibility and had already prepared a story together.

'I'm an old friend of the family,' said Cat, without raising so much as an eyebrow. 'I got to know Tom's mother through our membership of the Edinburgh Society for Women's Suffrage. I'm sure you're familiar with it?'

'Oh, er, of course,' said Fran unconvincingly.

'When Catherine told me that she and Hamish were planning to travel on the continent, I naturally offered to look after my godson during their absence.'

'Your godson?' Lou raised his eyebrows. 'You never mentioned that, Tom.'

'Didn't I?' Tom shrugged. 'Must have slipped my mind.'

'Tom has a tendency to miss out the important details,' said Cat. 'Now, Mr Stevenson,' she continued, taking control of the situation, as advised by Tom earlier. 'I must tell you that I have been absolutely loving the serial in *Young Folks* magazine.'

Lou looked shocked. 'You've read *that*?' he gasped. 'Oh, but it's only a frivolity, a story for children . . .'

'Tom first brought it to my attention,' said Cat. 'Naturally, I doubted that something of any stature might be found between those covers and yet, I was obliged to eat humble pie. I think you seriously underestimate it. I have been thrilled by what I've read so far and am already awaiting the next episode with baited breath. Let us not forget, that the things we read as babes in arms resonate with us for the rest of our days. And the *Wreck of the . . . the . . .*'

'*Hispaniola*,' Tom prompted her.

'Indeed, thank you, Tom. That story, Mr Stevenson, is something of lasting value. Why I shouldn't be surprised if it is still being read in fifty, a hundred . . . five hundred years from now!'

Lou swallowed. 'You honour me, Mrs McCallum. That, coming from the woman who wrote the *Path of Truth*, is a rare accolade indeed.' He shook his head. 'It's strange, because only this afternoon, as I worked upon the manuscript, I was suddenly filled with the sense that I was wasting my time, that nobody would accord such a simple tale anything more than it has already achieved.'

'Not so, Mr Stevenson. I am convinced of its genius, just as Tom is. But one thing is certain. It needs to be a book. And I would strongly urge you to proceed with that aim firmly in mind.'

For a moment, Lou seemed bereft of words. Then he recovered himself.

'Well, Catriona, if I may be so bold as to use your Christian name, I must introduce you to somebody who I know has been dying to meet you.' He looked at Tom and Fran. 'If you'll excuse us for a moment.' He led Cat across the room towards one of the huddles of people, leaving Tom standing rather awkwardly with Fran, who he had already discovered was of a more suspicious nature than her husband.

'So, you're Mrs McCallum's godson,' she murmured. 'How strange that she's never mentioned you before.'

'Cat's a busy woman,' said Tom, evasively.

'And how odd that the two of you are so convinced of Lou's genius. Almost as though you'd prearranged the conversation.'

Tom laughed nervously. 'Yeah, like that would happen,' he said.

'So you must have known Catriona's husband?'

'Oh, er, Josiah? Yeah, course I did. Nice bloke. And er, a great . . . a great bread-maker.'

'And such a shame what happened to him, don't you think?'

'Umm . . . yeah. Yeah, real shame.'

There was a long silence, while Fran studied him with interest. She seemed to be on the verge of asking another question, but then seemed to decide to let the matter pass. 'I'll get somebody to bring you a glass of cordial,' she said. She pointed. 'Lloyd is over there, talking to Mr Barrie.'

Tom looked in the direction she'd indicated and saw Lloyd lounging in a corner, chatting to a short, rather weedy-looking young man with black hair and a thick moustache. Lloyd appeared to be holding forth about something while Mr Barrie listened, a glum expression on his face. Tom sauntered over and nodded a greeting to Lloyd who glared at him, clearly far from happy to see him.

'Ah, who's this?' asked Mr Barrie, as though grateful to have some other company.

'This is the mysterious Tom Afflick,' said Lloyd, making no attempt to disguise the mocking tone in his voice. 'From Manchester, England. Tom, this is Mr Barrie.'

'A pleasure.' James shook Tom's hand. 'So what's so mysterious about you?' he asked.

'Oh, nothing really,' Tom assured him. 'Lloyd's just kidding around, aren't you Lloyd?'

But Lloyd wasn't giving in quite so easily. 'Tom appeared out of nowhere and started telling everyone what to do,' he said bluntly. 'Now he's got Papa running around like a dog with six legs, doing everything that Tom tells him.'

James smiled. 'Surely not?' he said.

'I'm just giving him a bit of advice about *Treasure Island*,' said Tom. He glared at Lloyd, challenging him to contradict the title, but he didn't. 'Mr Henley was telling me you're a bit of a writer too,' he said, trying to shift the spotlight away from himself.

'Oh, merely a dabbler,' insisted James. 'I've written a few drama reviews, but I intend to get more serious about it once I've graduated. I'm studying literature, of course.'

'So you're thinking of writing for children?'

'Oh, no.' James looked affronted. 'No, for adults. I'm not sure whether to write novels or plays.'

'I'm sure Tom will help you decide,' said Lloyd acidly.

Tom ignored him. 'Well, I think you should consider writing for kids, somewhere down the line,' he said.

'For *kids*?' muttered James, clearly intrigued. 'You mean children? What makes you say that?'

'Oh, I just have the feeling you'd be good at it.'

'See,' murmured Lloyd. 'What did I tell you. Mysterious.'

The evening proceeded agreeably enough. Tom eventually found himself standing with Cat at the back of the room, chatting quietly and making sly remarks about the other guests. Cat had also exchanged a few words with James Barrie and confided that she thought him a bit of a "wet blanket", whatever that was. She was amazed when Tom told her that Barrie too was destined for great success as a writer. She whispered that he didn't seem to have much of a character, that he seemed very immature. Tom thought about that and realised that maybe the story of Peter Pan was really all about the author.

Once the last guests had arrived and been given a drink, Fran announced to the room at large that the "entertainment" was about to begin. Lou took a seat at one end of the room, which had been kept clear of guests and opened a book. Everybody quietened down and Lou announced that he was going to read *Green Tea* by Sheridan Le Fanu. It turned out to be a short ghost story about a sea captain, living in Dublin, haunted by a mysterious dwarf who resembled somebody from the captain's troubled past. It was dark and atmospheric and Lou read with total conviction. When he'd spoken the last sentence there was a deep, appreciative silence and then a burst of polite applause. Lou smiled, closed the book and then looked around the room. 'I wonder,' he said, 'if I might persuade my good friend Mr William Henley to come up here and give us a reading of his wonderful poem, *Invictus*?'

William made a few modest protestations, but the crowd urged him to accept the challenge and so, after a few moments, he gamely hobbled to the top of the room and sat in the chair that Lou had just vacated. He waited in what appeared to be deep concentration and then began to recite a poem in his rich, resonant tones. It was only four verses long, but when he reached the final stanza, Tom was vaguely surprised to realise that he'd heard it somewhere before, though he couldn't say exactly where.

It matters not how strait the gate,
How charged with punishments the scroll,
I am the master of my fate,
I am the captain of my soul.

There was enthusiastic applause when he'd finished and William smiled and nodded his thanks around the room. Then he sat for a moment, looking at the other guests and Tom realized how this worked. The person who had just performed chose the next one in line. William's gaze swept around the room and then came to rest on Lloyd, who Tom noticed was grinning and preening as though eager to be the focus of everyone's attention.

'I wonder,' boomed William, 'if I might prevail upon young Lloyd to come up here and give us a reading of one of his favourites?'

Lloyd was up there like a shot, almost before William had finished talking and there was an awkward wait while the poet got himself upright and limped back to join the others. Lloyd stood for a moment, a grave expression on his face, ensuring that he had everyone's undivided attention and then announced in a very serious voice, 'I would now like to recite *Casabianca* by Mrs Felicia Hemans.' He paused. 'One of the finest poems ever written,' he added.

There were appreciative murmurs from the crowd and Tom supposed that this must be a particular favourite, though he didn't think he knew the poem. He glanced at Cat, but her gaze was, for the moment, fixed on Lloyd as he struck a dramatic pose and began his recitation.

The boy stood on the burning deck
Whence all but he had fled;
The flame that lit the battle's wreck
Shone round him o'er the dead.

Tom realized that he *had* heard the poem, or rather parodies of it, in his own era, where it seemed to have become an object of derision. He knew his father was fond of quoting a different version.

The boy stood on the burning deck.
His lips were all a quiver.
He gave a cough, his head dropped off
And floated down the river.

Whatever awaited it in the future, the poem was well received. Everyone listened with rapt attention. The problem was that Lloyd was over-egging it completely, speaking in a portentous tone and acting out every gesture in an exaggerated style, lifting a hand to his head, pointing at imagined clouds of smoke and pacing around the room like the unfortunate child in the poem. But when he reached the final lines, he was rewarded with more enthusiastic applause than his predecessors, together with cries of 'Bravo!' Lloyd bowed ostentatiously and then with that superior smirk on his face, he started scanning the onlookers, searching for a victim. Tom knew in that moment that he would be chosen next and he wondered what he might do to get out of it.

'Tom Afflick,' said Lloyd, still smirking. 'Mysterious Tom. Perhaps you'd like to step up here and give us one of *your* favourites?'

'Oh, er . . . I don't . . . I can't . . .' Tom tried to protest, but all around him people were urging him to take up the challenge and he didn't really see how he could avoid this without offending his hosts. He glanced helplessly at Cat and she gave him a steely look.

'Surely you're not going to back down?' she murmured. 'That's not the Tom I seem to remember.'

Tom sighed, lifted his hands in capitulation. He started walking though the audience and as he did so his mind was desperately turning over the possibilities. Poems? He didn't *know* any poems, apart from the bawdy ditties he sometimes heard from his friends, which frankly wouldn't be suitable for this occasion. So what then? There must be something he could do.

As he approached the chair where Lloyd was waiting, grinning mockingly at him, Tom noticed something resting against the wall beside the chair –

an acoustic guitar. He had what he thought might be a brainwave. He watched as Lloyd vacated the chair and swaggered back into the midst of the audience. Tom picked up the guitar, slung the strap around his neck and strummed a couple of chords. Luckily, it appeared to be more or less in tune. He looked around for Lou. 'Is it all right if I use this?' he asked.

'Of course,' said Lou, smiling. 'A musician too? Is there no end to your talents, Tom?'

Tom frowned. Calling him a musician was stretching a bit, since he only knew the one song. It wasn't even a particular favourite of his, but his dad loved it and often asked Tom to play it for him, especially when he'd had a pint or two. And Lloyd *had* asked for something from Manchester.

Tom took a deep breath and started strumming the rhythm. He hung back as long as he could, but finally decided he'd have to take the plunge. He started the first verse. His voice was thin but just about in tune, he thought and he tried not to register the puzzled expressions of the people watching him. But his voice strengthened when he hit the chorus and then he couldn't help but notice that amongst the crowd, heads were beginning to nod, feet were beginning to tap and then all of a sudden, people started clapping along. By the time he hit the second verse, everyone was joining in, everyone but Lloyd, who stood there with a furious scowl on his face.

Tom took it to the final chorus and by then he had the crowd virtually eating out of his hand. There were even voices joining in on the repeated chorus, even though the singers probably hadn't the faintest idea what a *Wonderwall* was or where they might expect to find one. The final chord died away to be replaced by an absolute torrent of heartfelt applause. Tom made a self-conscious bow, unslung the guitar and propped it back against the wall. He swung around and waited for the applause to die down, noticing with a hint of satisfaction that Lloyd was in the act of stalking out of the room, an expression of pure fury on his face.

Now it was Tom's turn to pick somebody and though he made a show of looking around the crowd he knew exactly who it was going to be.

'Catriona,' he said. 'I wonder if you remember a little song that you and your brother sang for me one time? *The Bird In The Hay*?'

Cat's face was a picture. For an instant it registered delight at the memory and then switched to a look of apprehension as she realised she was going to have to perform the song.

'Oh, I don't know if my poor voice is up to such a task,' she protested.

Tom gave her a look. 'Surely you're not going to back down?' he said. 'That's not the Cat I remember.'

She smiled then and urged on by those around her, she came forward to take Tom's place. As they passed each other, she took his hand for a moment and leaned close to whisper in his ear. 'This is the happiest night I've had in years,' she told him, and then they moved on past each other. Cat turned to look at her audience. She cleared her throat.

'The song that Tom refers to is a silly little ditty that

Fraser and I used to sing at the sessional school when we were bairns. It's no masterpiece and I'm no singer, but I trust you will forgive us both our considerable shortcomings.'

She closed her eyes for a moment and then began to sing.

The bird in the hay, one bright summer's day
He sang as he flew o'er the meadow.
Oh can't you all see, that I'm healthy and free
And I'm such a handsome young fellow?'

She'd been wrong about her voice, Tom decided. It was as sweet as ever. He remembered now, the last time she'd sung it for him and shortly afterwards how she'd told him that she believed his crazy stories of travelling in space and time. He'd wanted to kiss her then but had been uncomfortably aware of her brother watching them like a hawk; and now it occurred to him that such a moment would never come again, because he'd aged one year since then and she had aged more than fifty. He couldn't help feeling really sad about that.

The sound of applause brought him back to the present. Cat was bowing and smiling and thanking everyone for their kind appreciation. Her eyes met Tom's and he saw that they were full of tears and he knew exactly how she felt. His own eyes filled and he felt a gentle hand on his shoulder. He looked up and saw Fran gazing at him in concern.

'Why Tom, whatever's wrong?' she asked him.

He shrugged, shook his head. 'Memories,' he said.

She frowned. 'I don't really understand,' she murmured.

'Oh, yeah?' Tom wiped at his eyes with his sleeve. 'What's that?'

'Something that you said, just now. That Miss McCallum and her *brother* sang that song for you. But, forgive me, I understood her brother died a very long time ago. I would have thought . . . before you were even born?'

Tom stared at her. He had no answer for that.

'I think I'll get myself another glass of cordial,' he said, and hurried away.

Fourteen

The party broke up around midnight. The Stevensons had engaged the services of a whole row of hansom cabs to take their guests to their homes and one by one, people were called out to the hallway to say goodbye to their hosts. When it came to Tom and Cat's turn, he noticed that there was no sign of Lloyd. Fran explained that the boy had felt tired and had gone to his room, but Tom felt sure he just hadn't liked being overshadowed by Tom's performance. The thought that Lloyd might be annoyed with him made him distinctly nervous.

'You are a constant surprise,' Lou told Tom, as a manservant helped him on with his coat. 'That song you performed, I can honestly say I've never heard anything like it.' Lou had consumed quite a bit of whisky over the evening and was what Tom's dad liked to describe as 'well-oiled'.

'Oh, it's just an old Manchester thing,' Tom assured him. 'Seriously, you hear nothing else round my way.'

'I must see if I can get the sheet music. Who is the composer?'

'Erm, he's called Noel Gallagher. But I don't think it'll be available just yet. Not for quite a while, actually.'

Lou turned his attention to Cat. 'And your performance, too, Mrs McCallum. A real joy. Thank you so much for sharing it.' He leaned a little closer, as if to confess a secret. 'You know, I must confess, I had always thought of you as a much more *serious* person. But after tonight, I've realised that some people have hidden depths.'

'Thank you, I'm sure,' said Cat. 'I believe it's Tom who brings out my more playful nature. It's wonderful to have him back.'

'He's been away?' murmured Fran, suspiciously. She had been asking awkward questions all night, her suspicions clearly aroused.

'Umm, well, not "away" exactly. It's just been a while since we've been able to spend time together. I'm afraid I've been somewhat lax in my duties as a godmother.' She took Lou's hands in hers. 'Well, Mr Stevenson, it has been a splendid evening, I have enjoyed myself immensely.' She fixed him with a commanding look. 'Now, please don't forget. *Treasure Island*. It is destined to be a book and I feel sure that with application, it *will* be. But that all depends on you.'

Tom was aware of Fran looking on suspiciously as Cat spoke, so he took her arm and led her towards the open doorway. 'We must be on our way,' he announced. 'Merry Christmas everyone!'

'Merry Christmas, Tom,' shouted Lou, too drunk

to notice anything amiss, but Tom was aware of Fran gazing after them as they went out of the door.

'Something wrong?' murmured Cat.

'We don't want to lay it on too thick,' said Tom. 'Fran's as sharp as a knife, I think she knows we're up to some . . .' He broke off in surprise. It was snowing, big thick flakes drifting down from the heavens.

'How lovely,' murmured Cat. 'Just in time for Christmas.'

They crossed the pavement to the hansom cab, the door of which was being held open by another manservant. Tom hesitated and looked suspiciously up at the cabbie, sitting at the back. The man's face was covered with a scarf, so Tom gestured to him to reveal it, which he did, looking puzzled. But the face beneath the scarf was perfectly normal, so Tom turned back and helped Cat climb up into the cab.

'What was that about?' she murmured as Tom perched himself on the seat opposite her.

'Just not taking any chances,' he told her. 'I had a dodgy ride in one of these things the other night.'

'Dodgy?' The word was clearly unfamiliar to her.

'Unsafe,' he elaborated.

They heard the sound of the cabbie clicking his tongue and the hansom cab moved away at a more leisurely speed than on Tom's previous trip.

'Do you think we managed to persuade Lou to continue with his book?' asked Cat anxiously.

'I hope so,' said Tom. Then an idea occurred to him. 'Let's check,' he suggested. He reached into the pocket of his coat and pulled out the sheets of paper that he'd left there. It was hard to be sure in the uncertain light of the cab, but he could see that once again, all the pages had some kind of content on them. 'I think we're ok,' he said. 'I'll check again when the light's a bit better.'

Cat shook her head. 'I don't really understand what those pages represent,' she said.

'It's kind of hard to explain,' said Tom. 'You see, in the future, there's a thing called the World Wide Web. It's like . . . it's like an invisible rope that links people all over the globe. So, I can sit at a computer in Manchester and you could be on another computer in Edinburgh.' He noticed the look on her face. 'A computer is a machine that . . . well, it's kind of like a mechanical brain that can hold all this knowledge – every bit of information that's ever been thought of in the entire history of the world . . . and I can tap into it any time I want to find out about something –' He was struggling now and he tried to think of an example. 'Well, you take *The Path of Truth*, for instance. I read about it in the museum and I wanted to read the book. But I was told it was out of print. So I went to my computer and I typed in the name and there it was.'

'Where was it?' asked Cat, mystified.

'Just sort of floating around on something called Project Gutenberg. And I was able to pull the pages down onto my screen and . . .' He shook his head. He realised there was no way that he could ever make her understand such a thing. The truth was, he didn't really understand how it worked himself. He waved the printed sheets. 'These pages tell us things that are going to happen in the future,' he said and decided that for the time being, it was the best he was going to be able to manage. He made an attempt to change the subject. 'Hey, that was a great party, wasn't it?'

Cat smiled. 'I really enjoyed it. The Stevensons are a delightful family, don't you think?' She studied him for a moment. 'Though I have to confess that Lou's stepson is a bit of a handful. I'll hazard a guess and say that the two of you aren't really the best of friends.'

Tom nodded. 'He's so full of himself. Did you see him, doing that poem? He thought he was Benedict flipping Cumberbatch.'

'He thought he was *what*?'

'It's a "who", not a "what". An actor, back in my time. Thinks he's "it". And so does Lloyd.' He frowned. 'Trouble is, he knows all about me now. He's the only one who does, apart from you.'

'Was it wise, telling him?'

'No, it wasn't. But I sort of had to. I was in a fix.'

'And it worries you that he knows?'

'Yes. See, I can trust you but Lloyd . . . well, he's such a div.'

'A div?'

'Yeah, you know. A fruitcake. A dimmock. A spod.'

Cat smiled. 'I'm beginning to wish I'd brought my notebook,' she said. 'I'd forgotten about all your funny little expressions.'

'Yes, well, all I'm saying is, the first time Lloyd's not happy about something, he's going to tell Lou and Fran. And I don't know what will happen, if he does that.'

'What's the worst that could happen?'

Tom sighed. 'Well, let's see. He'll get Lou all mixed up in it. Lou will forget about those revisions on *Treasure Island*. It'll never get published as a book. Lou won't become a famous writer. And it'll be all my fault.'

Cat nodded. 'That *is* an appalling prospect,' she agreed. She sighed. 'So, what's the answer?'

Tom frowned. 'I suppose we could always murder Lloyd.' He saw the expression on Cat's face and shook his head. 'Only kidding,' he added.

'Well, thank goodness for that! Lloyd's undoubtedly a brat but I don't think he deserves that.'

'No. Tempting though, isn't it?'

She looked at him for a moment. 'You *are* joking, I suppose?'

'Yeah, of course.' But they both chuckled at the idea.

They heard the coachman say 'whoah' and the cab slowed to a halt. Tom threw open the door and leaned out. He looked both ways to ensure that the coast was clear before jumping down. Then he helped Cat to descend. She gave a soft grunt of exertion as she stepped down onto the pavement.

'Look at me,' she muttered. 'A few hours on my feet and I'm almost crippled. Oh, to be your age again.' She opened her purse, took out a coin and gave it to Tom to hand up to the cabbie. The man tipped his hat and wished them both a Merry Christmas. He snapped the whip and the coach moved briskly away. Tom and Cat stood for a moment, looking at the silent snow descending from above. The road was already covered beneath a mantle of pure white, which glistened in the light of the street lamps.

'How lovely,' murmured Cat. 'I can't remember when it last snowed on Christmas Day.' She led the way towards the front door of the house and as they approached it swung open and there was Angus, waiting for them, standing smartly to attention. It occurred to Tom that he must have been hanging around in the hall all evening, waiting for his mistress's return. Cat and Tom climbed the steps to the door.

'I trust you had a good evening, madam?' said Angus.

'Very enjoyable, thank you.'

'Can I get you anything? Tea, perhaps, or hot milk?'

'No, thank you.'

Angus leaned closer. 'The little errand you sent me out on earlier?' he murmured. 'It's on the table in the drawing room.'

Cat looked confused for a moment and then seemed to remember something. 'Ah yes, I'd quite forgotten! You managed it all right?'

'Yes, madam. It took a little persuasion, what with it being the last day before the holidays, but I think you'll be pleased with the results.'

'Excellent. Well, now, Angus, why don't you take yourself off home? Tom and I will happily see to ourselves. And mind you don't come back until after Boxing Day.'

'Very good, madam. Thank you.' Angus bowed politely and moved off along the hall. Tom and Cat hung up their coats and walked to the drawing room. As Tom dropped onto the sofa, he couldn't help but notice a small package wrapped in bright paper lying on the low table in front of him. Cat gestured to it. 'That's for you,' she said. 'It's your Christmas present.'

Tom looked at her. 'Oh, there was no need to get me anything,' he protested.

She smiled and settled herself beside him. 'I realise that,' she said. 'But I wanted to. After all, it's not every day that an old friend comes visiting. And I had to act quickly. I sent Angus off this afternoon with strict instructions. I hope he managed to get exactly what I asked for.'

Tom smiled and picked up the package. 'Can I open it now?' he asked.

'Of course. It's Christmas Day. What better time?'

Tom frowned. 'I haven't anything to give you,' he told her.

'But you've already given me the best Christmas present I could have hoped for,' she insisted. 'Just by being here.'

They gazed at each other for a moment and Tom thought how incredibly sad it was. They could be no more than good friends now, but when they had last met, it had seemed to him that it was going to be something more than that.

'Thanks,' he said, at last, and he tore the paper from the package, to find a leather-bound box within. He opened it and saw, resting on a cushion of black velvet, a round silver object on a length of chain. He removed it from the box and noticed that the front of it was hinged. He pressed a catch and the front flipped open, revealing a beautiful pocket watch. He couldn't withhold a gasp of delight. Then he noticed that the inside of the cover had been inscribed in an elegant, ornate hand. He studied the message in silence.

To Tom
For the good times
Merry Christmas
Cat

'It's beautiful,' he whispered and despite himself, his eyes filled with tears.

It seemed the most appropriate thing,' said Cat. 'It needed to be small enough to carry with you. And what better gift for a boy who has conquered time? As for the message, well, I didn't want to put a date on it or anything else you'd have trouble explaining away. When you go back, I mean. So . . .'

He could see that she too was close to tears. He reached out and squeezed her hand. 'I'm sorry,' he said. 'I wish I could change things, but I can't.'

'It *is* a cruel trick that time has played on us,' she said. She forced a brave smile. 'But, rather this, Tom, than I went to my grave without ever seeing you again. That would have been crueler still, don't you agree?'

He nodded. He couldn't think of anything else to say, so they sat there, the two of them in companionable silence, while beyond the big bay window behind them, the snow continued to fall.

*

He went to bed that night in Cat's guest room,

luxuriously furnished with a big four poster bed and velvet drapes, a far cry from some of the places he'd been obliged to spend the night on his previous visits. He remembered one bed in particular, under the eaves of the orphanage in Mary King's Close. He'd been forced to share the grimy, narrow bed with Cameron, in a grubby gloomy little attic room where rats scampered wherever they felt like going.

Cat hadn't had any men's pyjamas in the house, so Tom had simply removed his shoes and socks and climbed into the huge bed wearing his t-shirt and jeans.

He was tired but for the moment at least, he couldn't seem to get to sleep. A hundred conflicting thoughts were twisting and turning in his head and he didn't have the first idea about how to settle any of the problems that assailed him. After a while, he turned onto his side and reached for the pocket watch, which lay on the bedside cabinet beside him. He flipped open the case and examined it fondly in the dim light from the window. As he did so, he noticed something odd. The hands of the clock had started to move, slowly at first, but with increasing speed. And then it occurred to him that they were actually moving backwards. *What now?* he thought, with a calmness that surprised him.

His surroundings began to turn grey and transparent and a dizziness filled his head. Then he heard a familiar noise, the sound of wings, beating all around him. He didn't know where he was headed, but one thing was for sure. Judging by the hands of the clock he was going even further back in time.

And then he was gone, falling down a long twisting tunnel and he seemed to fall for a very long time before he finally hit the ground.

Fifteen

His feet thudded onto soft earth and he rocked on his heels for an instant, disorientated, flinging his arms into the air to try and regain his balance. Everything around him rushed suddenly into focus and a series of vivid impressions assailed him. It was bright daylight and a cold wind was clawing at him, chilling him to the bone because he wasn't wearing a coat. The smell of the outdoors was in his nostrils, the odours of grass, mud and rain. Overhead, a grey, stormy sky tumbled and roiled in silent fury.

He managed to steady himself and lowered his arms, noting with a dull sense of surprise that he was still holding the silver pocket watch. When he looked at it closely, he saw that the hands were no longer moving in the wrong direction. They were positioned at a little after half past two.

Now he registered that his feet felt cold and wet and when he looked down, he saw to his surprise that they were bare, just as they had been in the bed in Cat's spare room. That was it then. He'd gone straight from there to this outdoor location. He turned his head to look around him and knew instantly where he was – standing on the steep slope of Arthur's Seat, close to the place where he and a younger Cat had buried the tiny coffins. As the thought occurred to him, he looked down the slope and his heart lurched in his chest as he saw a familiar figure, making her way down the hillside away from him. Even from this distance her long blonde hair was unmistakable.

'Cat!' he yelled. She paused and looked back over her shoulder, gazing up at him in surprise. Then she lifted a hand to wave frantically at him and turning, she began to make her way upwards again. He pushed the watch safely into his pocket and started towards her, having to place his bare feet with care on the precarious, rock-pitted terrain, but he was in such a hurry to get to her that it made him clumsy. At the last moment, a combination of a stubbed toe and his own impetus caused him to lose his balance. He crashed into her, throwing his arms around her as he did so and the two of them went tumbling back down the hillside, rolling over several times before coming to a rude halt, propped against a large, grey boulder.

'Ow,' said Cat, quietly. They lay for a moment, both of them panting with exertion, as they stared imploringly into each other's eyes. Then, 'Where did you go to?' she asked him, breaking the spell. 'I was so worried about you.'

Reluctantly, he released her and sat up. 'How long was I gone?'

'About a quarter of an hour,' she said and he could

see now that she'd been crying, her lovely green eyes rimmed with red. 'I didn't know what had happened to you. You just . . . it was as though you were suddenly made of smoke. I tried to grab you but then you were gone. I'd given up hope. I thought I'd never see you again.'

He smiled, though he didn't feel that there was all that much to smile about. He had no idea what was happening. He was puzzled. This was a new experience. Usually he stayed fixed in the same time-frame, slipping backwards and forwards between it and his own world. Why had he been sent back here, to a time he'd already visited earlier? And how long would he be allowed to stay?

'Where did you go?' Cat asked again.

'Well, that's a long story,' he warned her.

'Tell me anyway,' she suggested.

'Ok. Well, first I went back to my own time,' he said. 'I hooked up with my dad. He took me back to Manchester and I went on with my life. You know, school, friends, stuff like that.'

'Tom, how is that possible? You were only gone for fifteen minutes.'

He shook his head. 'It might have seemed like it to you, but it was actually more than a year.'

'A year?' She shook her head. 'Surely not?'

'Oh, yes, believe it. A lot happened to me. But then, I came back to Edinburgh to visit my mum and I was in this car . . .' He thought for a moment. 'You remember the coaches I told you about? The ones that don't need horses?'

She nodded.

'Well, I was travelling in one of those and I saw this magpie . . .'

'Where? In the coach?'

'No, it was sitting on a rail. It was night-time and I thought it seemed really weird, you know? And anyway, there was this accident and the car went off the road. The next thing I knew, I was back again, only this time it was 1881.'

She stared at him. 'But, it's only 1829 now!'

'I know how it sounds. But that's where I was taken . . . and . . . I met this writer. A guy called Robert Louis Stevenson; don't worry, you won't have heard of him, not yet, but he will be famous in my time. And you'll meet him too, one day, he'll be a friend. Also . . .' He hesitated, not sure that he should tell her any more.

'Go on,' she urged him.

'Well, I met somebody else in 1881. Somebody I already knew. I . . .' His voice trailed off. 'I met you,' he said.

She actually laughed at that. 'But, how could you? I'm *here*.'

'Yes, but you were there too. As . . . as an old woman.'

There was a long silence then, while she thought it through.

'How old?' she asked at last.

He did the maths in his head. 'Around seventy,' he said.

'I was *seventy*. And you were still the same?'

He nodded.

'Well, that's terrible! I shouldn't like that one little bit.'

'No, I don't think either of us did.' He reached out and took one of her hands in his. 'But the thing is, Cat, you'll be a rich woman by then, living in a fancy house with servants and everything. And you'll have books.'

'I have quite a few now.'

'No, I mean books you've *written*.'

'Never!' she protested.

'Oh, trust me, it's going to happen.' He smiled at her. 'I've seen it, Cat. Even back in my own time. It was all in a big museum. There was a painting of you and all your notebooks and stuff. Seriously, you're going to be remembered.'

She bowed her head and looked at her hands. 'But that's insane,' she muttered.

'You *do* believe me, don't you?' he asked her.

She looked up at him and smiled. 'Of course,' she said. 'Though it's a little hard to understand.' She pointed at him. 'But now I can see you must have been gone longer than I thought. Your clothes are completely different. Your hair's shorter. And . . .' She studied his bare feet, clearly baffled.

'I was in bed,' he explained. 'I was in a bed in your house.' He thought for a moment. 'Whoah!' he said.

'What's the matter?'

'I'm just thinking, it's a good job I had some clothes on!'

They both laughed at that.

'Imagine if you'd turned up in your night shirt!' cried Cat.

'That's just the problem. You didn't have anything like that. So I just took off my shoes and socks and climbed in to bed. Thank goodness I left my jeans and t-shirt on or I could have arrived here in just my socks and gruds.'

'Your *what*?'

'Never mind.' Tom remembered something else. He reached into his pocket and pulled out the silver pocket watch. 'Have a look at this,' he said. 'Do you like it?'

'I do,' she told him.

'You ought to. You gave it to me.' He flipped open the case and indicated the inscription. 'See that? You're going to give me this on Christmas Day, 1881. It's going to snow and we'll just have come back from a party at a famous writer's house. What do you think of that?'

Cat laughed delightedly at the notion. 'It sounds like a dream,' she told him.

'It does, doesn't it? But it's going to happen, Cat. You'll see. Just give it about . . . fifty-five years.'

Her expression turned serious. 'I don't want to, Tom. Not if it means I won't see you again until then.'

He shrugged, took the watch back from her and returned it to his pocket.

'We don't get any say over this,' he told her. 'That's not the way it works. But we're together now, and that's what matters. We should make the most of it.'

She smiled demurely. 'I can't imagine what you mean,' she said. 'I hope you're not thinking of being unchivalrous.' She said it, but her eyes told him a different story. He reached out to her but paused when he noticed that she was looking over his shoulder at something behind him. Her face registered surprise. 'Who's that?' she asked.

He turned to look and his heart nearly stopped beating in his chest. A cloaked figure was coming down the hillside towards them. The figure of a man, tall and angular, silhouetted against the skyline, his head hidden behind a crow-like mask.

'Oh, no!' whispered Tom. In an instant, he was on his feet and dragging Cat up after him. 'We have to go,' he said.

'But . . .'

'NOW!' He started down the hillside, pulling her along with him, wincing every time his bare feet settled on a sharp piece of rock.

'But who is it?'

'You remember I told you about the man who's following me?' he grunted. 'The bad man?' But he was unsure, for the moment, which version of Cat he had told. 'He wants to harm me. You too, probably, if he catches up with us.'

He increased his pace, pulling her after him. The incline was still steep and they were going faster and faster. He worried abut falling again, but when he looked back over his shoulder he could see that McSweeny was following them at a loping run, his leather cloak flapping behind him like the wings of a huge bat. He was gaining on them so Tom increased his pace.

'Tom, slow down!' cried Cat. 'I can't, I can't keep up with you.'

He didn't dare do as she asked. He was terrified what McSweeny might do to her if he caught them. He remembered Morag and what had happened to her at the market in Mary King's Close. In his mind's eye he saw McSweeny's arm encircling her, the knife blade glittering dangerously in his free hand. Tom couldn't let something like that happen to Cat. He *wouldn't*.

So he ran as fast as he could and even as he ran he was aware of a mounting dizziness in his head, the world greying out around him, his bare feet no longer making real contact with the stony ground beneath him. And then, a short distance ahead of him, further down the hill, he noticed a shape flapping up into the air, the black and white outline of a magpie. It occurred to him that he really should let go of Cat's hand now, but to do that would be to leave her here at McSweeny's mercy and he knew he couldn't risk it. So he kept a tight hold of her. And then everything was beyond his control as the greyness overtook him completely, and once again he felt himself falling, but even as he fell, he was still aware of one solid thing: Cat's hand gripped tightly in his.

*

He hurtled face down onto a yielding softness, a cool, embracing softness that he instantly recognised as a mattress. An instant later another body came crashing down on top of him, making him gasp for breath as the air was driven out of his lungs. Whoever had fallen onto him grunted loudly, rolled to one side and fell off the edge of the bed. There was a fierce exclamation as a body thudded down onto bare wooden floorboards. Tom grabbed a quick breath then scrambled to the edge of the four-poster and peered fearfully over it. Cat was lying on her back on the floor, staring up at him in open-mouthed astonishment.

'Tom,' she gasped. 'What . . .? Where . . . where are we?'

He was about to answer the question when the door of the room creaked open and there stood Old Cat, dressed in a white nightgown and staring in at him, a baffled expression on her face. 'Tom,' she said. 'I just remembered something. I can't imagine how I forgot but it came back to me, all of a sudden. I *did* see you again. Just after you disappeared from Arthur's Seat, you came back, only for a few moments and there was this strange man in a cloak . . .' She broke off and her eyes widened. Tom realised that she was staring at his bare feet. He looked down at them and saw that they were filthy. Matted with a mixture of dirt and blood, they had stained the white bedcovers.

'What on earth happened to you?' gasped Cat.

Just then, Young Cat sat up and peeped wide-eyed over the edge of the bed. The woman and the girl stared at each other in mute disbelief, across a distance of more than fifty years. Tom lay there between them, wondering what would be the best way to handle this. Finally, he twisted around and sat up, then looked from Old Cat to Young Cat and back again.

'Hey guys,' he said quietly. 'I'd like to introduce you to er . . . yourselves.'

Nobody said anything for quite a while after that.

Sixteen

It was the early hours of Christmas morning but sleep seemed a long way off. They sat at the kitchen table, the three of them, sipping at cups of tea, which Old Cat had been obliged to make herself since all the staff had gone home for the holidays. They sat there in silence while they tried to make sense of what had just happened. The two Cats were seated at either end of the table, staring intently at each other while Tom sat rather sheepishly between them, wondering how in the world he was going to sort this little mess out.

It was Old Cat who spoke first.

'I'd quite forgotten how pretty you were,' she said. 'Such lovely skin. And that beautiful blonde hair. What I wouldn't give to have that now.'

Young Cat smiled feebly. 'Thank you,' she said. 'And you look . . .'

'Ancient,' finished Old Cat. 'An absolute fright, I should imagine.' She chuckled grimly. 'I realise it must be a shock for you, seeing yourself like this. It's not something I would have wished for at your age.

At *any* age, come to think of it.' She looked at Tom helplessly. 'I don't really understand how this is even possible,' she said.

Tom shrugged his shoulders. 'Join the club,' he muttered.

Old Cat gave him an exasperated look, so he tried to explain further. 'I suppose it's because I hung onto you, I mean, *her*. When I was coming back. And I must have just dragged her – you – along with me.'

'But, aren't there rules about this kind of thing?' asked Young Cat.

'Rules?' Tom looked at her blankly. 'I don't know about any rules. I haven't got a clue what I'm doing. These things just happen to me and I have to go along with them, the best way I can. If there are rules, I haven't made head nor tail of them.'

'Well, I take your point, Tom,' said Old Cat, sternly, 'but the question is, how are we going to get her – me – back again?'

'Get her back?'

'Yes. Well she can't stay here, can she? How would I ever explain her presence? People are sure to notice that I now have a younger version of myself living in the same house.'

'True,' agreed Tom.

'And the other thing is, she's going to be missed back in her own time. Her – *our* parents. And Fraser, of course. They're probably already wondering where she's got to.'

Tom nodded. 'I understand what you're saying,' he said. 'But, I haven't got the first idea about how to get her back.' He looked from one to the other of them. 'I'm sorry,' he told them both.

'And . . . forgive me, dear . . .' Old Cat glanced at her younger self apologetically. 'If she doesn't get back to her own time, what's going to happen to *me*? I mean, everything will change, won't it? I might not be the person I am now if this is allowed to continue much longer.'

'Yes, I can see that,' said Tom. He thought of the way he'd explained time to Lloyd. A line of dominoes, falling over and knocking each other down. But he'd unwittingly removed a really important domino from the line and if he didn't get it back into position soon, who knew where it would end?'

'Maybe . . .' he said.

They both looked at him intently.

'I'm thinking that if we go back to where it happened – to Arthur's Seat? And, well, maybe we could try and set up the same situation again . . . you know, the two of us running downhill together. Only this time, I'd let go of her hand.' He glanced at Young Cat. '*Your* hand,' he elaborated. 'You see, that's how I think I went back to 1829 in the first place. I was like thinking about you and wishing I could go back to explain what had happened. So we could be the same age again.' He glanced at Old Cat. 'No offence,' he said.

'None taken.'

'So maybe if we were in the same location, and I wished that you would go back to your own time. Maybe, maybe I could send you there. Would that work?'

'It's got to be worth a try,' said Young Cat. 'Except . . .'

'Except what?' asked Tom.

'What if I'd rather stay here . . . with you?'

Tom stared at her. He didn't know what to say to that.

'That's really not an option,' said Old Cat, sternly. 'Think about it, my dear. Think of the possible repercussions. I am who I am now because of the life you've lived. You have to live that same life, just as it was intended to be in order to end up here, now, as *me*. You have to grow up, meet your future husband . . .'

Young Cat pulled a face. 'I always thought I'd never marry,' she said.

'Well, so did I.' Old Cat waved a hand in exasperation. 'Of course I did. We're the same, you and me.' She thought for a moment. 'I thought that way until I met Tom. Then everything changed.'

Young Cat looked at him. 'And then I told myself that there was only one person I'd *ever* marry,' she murmured.

'Er, do you have to talk about me as though I'm not here?' muttered Tom.

'Wheesht,' said Old Cat. She turned back to her younger self. 'Some things are just not meant to be, my dear. You will meet a good man in time and you will marry him.'

'And I'll be happy with that?' asked Young Cat.

'Yes. Tolerably so.' Old Cat smiled. 'When you are older, you'll have realised that life doesn't always give you exactly what you want. That you settle for something else, even if it isn't your heart's desire. After Tom left, I was devastated, of course I was, but, well, that didn't last forever. Time heals all wounds, isn't that what they say? And I came to realise that it could never have worked, no matter how I felt about him.'

Tom felt distinctly uncomfortable. He wished they'd start talking about something else.

Young Cat gestured at her surroundings. 'And all this will be waiting for me down the line? The fine house, the servants?'

'Yes. But you'll also come to realise that they don't really matter. They're just the means to an end. Having all this allowed me to do the things I really wanted to do. To write my books, to devote myself to the causes I believed in. In the end, isn't that what we really want, my dear? The freedom to be the person we've always believed we *can* be?'

Young Cat nodded. 'I suppose so,' she said.

'Good. Well, drink up your tea, the two of you. Tom, I would suggest that you make your way to Arthur's Seat just as soon as it's light enough. The less time we keep Catriona away from her family, the better.' She set down her cup and got to her feet. 'And now, I'll leave the two of you alone. I'm sure you have a lot to talk about before she goes back.'

'But we don't even know if it will work,' Tom reminded her.

'I have a feeling it will.' Old Cat smiled mysteriously. 'I think it *does* work, Tom. Don't ask me what makes me think that, but I have a good feeling about it. Perhaps even the faintest memory of it happening.'

'And you think she'll get back safely?' persisted Tom. She nodded.

'What about McSweeny? He could still be there, waiting for her.'

'The man in the cloak?' Old Cat shook her head. 'I don't think he'll be there. I imagine I'll find myself standing on the hillside alone again.' She looked at her younger self. 'I'm sorry, my dear. You will shed tears over this parting. And I don't know if you will remember everything that has happened here. If you do, then you will look forward to Christmas Eve, 1881, because you'll know that is when you will meet Tom again. I'm afraid, if that is the case, it will have taken the surprise out of it but I suppose there's a lot to be said for anticipation.'

Young Cat smiled at her older self. 'It's been nice meeting you,' she said.

'And for me also. I'd like very much to give you a hug, just now, but I'm afraid to even try such a thing. So I'll let Tom do that for me. Goodnight, the two of you. Tom, wrap up warm to go up that hill. And for goodness sake, put some shoes on!'

She went out of the kitchen, leaving them alone at the table. Tom looked at Young Cat. 'Are you all right?' he asked her.

She nodded. She took his hand and squeezed it tightly. 'How long do we have?' she asked him. 'Before it gets light?' He reached into his pocket and pulled out the watch, flipped open the silver case. 'An hour or so,' he said.

'Let's not waste any of it,' she said. She reached out, put her arms around him and pulled him close.

*

They set out at dawn. The snow was still falling and a pristine, white covering crunched beneath their feet. They didn't say much as they walked, both of them preferring to think about what had happened between them in the kitchen, both of them dreading the separation to come. There was nobody else around. When they finally left the outskirts of the city and reached the lower slopes of Arthur's Seat, the going became increasingly tough, but they toiled upwards, knowing exactly where they were headed. The hillside looked somewhat different under its mantle of snow and it took them quite a while to find the exact place where they'd buried the coffins. The little sealed-off area was open to the elements now, its precious contents long gone.

'Nobody ever remembered exactly where the coffins were found,' Tom told Cat. 'When I read about it in my time, there were just theories, but nobody was really sure exactly which part of the hill they were hidden on.' He smiled, remembering. 'Fraser worked so hard on those things,' he said.

'We all did,' murmured Cat.

The mention of Cat's brother reminded Tom about something. 'Promise me one thing,' he said. 'When you get back – *if* you get back – if you ever hear that Fraser is planning to join the army, do your best to talk him out of it.'

She looked at him. 'Ach, you know Fraser,' she told him. 'He's as stubborn as a mule. Of course he wants to join the army. He's never wanted anything more than that.' She looked at him intently. 'Is there something I need to know?'

'Just that . . . oh, he'd be better off if he does something else. And if you can't stop him from joining up, at least tell him to stay away from Africa.'

'You're being very mysterious,' she complained.

'I'm sorry,' he said. 'I don't think I should say any more. Just remember. Not Africa.'

She nodded. It was very quiet up on the snowbound hillside.

They turned and looked downhill. 'I think we were just down there,' said Tom, pointing. 'Past those rocks.'

She nodded. She was shivering, despite the thick shawl draped around her shoulders. 'Hold me for a moment,' she whispered. He did as she asked, aware of her heart beating next to his. He realised then how much he wanted her to stay, even though he knew he couldn't let her.

'I didn't get a chance last time,' he murmured. 'To tell you how I really felt about you.'

She looked up at him. 'Don't say anything now,' she urged him. 'It will only make it harder to go back.'

He nodded. He gave her a last fierce hug, then released her and took her left hand in his. They gazed down the hill. Now it had come to it, this seemed like the most ridiculous idea he had ever come up with. But Old Cat had seemed pretty sure it would work and he certainly didn't have any better ideas. As he stared down the hill, he saw a sudden swirl of black and white feathers, as a magpie swooped down and perched on a rock up ahead of them, something that made him feel that perhaps this *was* the right thing to do. The magpie had something to do with all this shifting around in time, of that he was sure. 'Ready?' he asked Young Cat.

She nodded. He saw that she was crying now, her shoulders moving up and down, but she somehow managed to stay silent.

'Let's go,' he said. And they began to run down the hill, slipping and sliding on the treacherous ground. For a moment he didn't think anything was going to happen. But he willed her to go back and then, as they sped up, he felt the greyness returning and had to remind himself that he needed to let go of her hand this time, though there was a part of him that wanted to hang on to her forever, to hang on tight and never let her go.

He was dimly aware of the magpie launching itself into the sky, up ahead of them.

'Tom!' he heard Cat gasp. 'Tom, do it now!' He steeled himself. He was moving at speed and was no longer aware of his feet crunching into the snow-covered ground beneath him. 'Goodbye,' he croaked and opened his hand.

And she was gone. Quite suddenly, without so much as a puff of smoke or a flash of light, she had slipped through the fabric of time and he was running on alone. He willed himself not to follow her, to stay here in the time that had claimed him and somehow, he managed it. The greyness around him began to draw more colour into itself. He slowed, stumbled, fell to his knees and slid several yards until he thumped to a halt against a boulder. Then he twisted around and looked back the way he had come. He saw a trail of footprints leading back up the hill and a short distance further on, a place where two sets of prints, running side-by-side had suddenly become one. A powerful sadness welled up in his chest, making him gasp. He threw back his head, gazed up into the snow-filled clouds and yelled out her name, once. He heard the echoes of his call rolling down the hillside, unanswered, and knew that she could not reach him now, that the girl he had loved was gone and he would never meet her again, at least, not in that form.

He bowed his head and got back to his feet, stood for a while on the deserted hillside, waiting for something that he knew would never come. Finally, he shrugged his coat tighter around him and sobbing, started back down the hill, alone.

*

When he got back to Lauriston Street and rang the doorbell, it was Old Cat who answered. She stood in the doorway for a moment, looking at him, then stepped aside to let him in. He stood in the hallway with his back to her, while she closed the door.

'Tell me what happened,' he said gently. 'When you got back.'

'Nothing,' she assured him. 'There was nobody else around. I stood on the hillside for a while, hoping you'd reappear but you didn't. After an hour or so, I finally admitted defeat. I walked home. I never spoke of it to my parents or to Fraser.'

'Fraser.' Tom remembered something. 'Did you manage to persuade him?'

'I tried. But he wouldn't listen to me. I even tried telling him the truth but he would have none of it. He said I was crazy, that meeting you had addled me. So he enlisted in the army and he ended up dying in that same African war. Only it was worse this time, much worse, because I knew it was going to happen one day and there was nothing I could do to change it.'

Tom studied his boots for a while. 'It's a lie,' he said.

'What is?'

'You see these movies about time-travel and it all looks like its going to be such good fun. But most of the time, it just sucks.'

'Tom, I'm so sorry,' she murmured. 'If there was a way I thought we could have made it work, I would have done it. But you know that she . . . that *I*, had to go back, don't you?'

He nodded.

'Can I get you anything? A drink? Something to eat?'

He shook his head. 'I'm going back to bed,' he said, his voice expressionless. And he went upstairs to the spare room. He pulled off his coat and dropped it onto the floor. He kicked off his shoes. On the mattress, he saw something that Young Cat had left behind: a length of red ribbon. It must have fallen from her hair, he decided, when she'd first crashed down onto the bed. He picked it up and inhaled it, thinking that it still held the faintest trace of her scent. He felt as empty as an old bottle. He lay down on the bed, held the ribbon to his face and fell into a deep and dreamless sleep.

Seventeen

'Tom, are you ever going to get out of that bed?'

Mum's voice woke him, sounding more than a little bit testy. He opened his eyes, blinking around the room. It took him just a couple of moments to establish that he was back in the spare room in Fairmilehead. He shook his head and sat up, pushing back the covers. He wasn't surprised to find that he was fully dressed, apart from his shoes, which he saw were lying a short distance away, caked in dried mud. He swung his legs over the side of the bed and sat there, feeling distinctly groggy.

His bedroom door opened a chink and he saw Mum peeping cautiously in. She registered surprise. 'You *are* up,' she said. 'Did you sleep in your clothes?'

Tom shrugged. 'Er, I suppose I must have,' he muttered.

'Well, get your backside into gear. We've got a few things to do before we start getting ready for tonight.'

He looked at her, puzzled. 'Tonight?' he echoed.

'The concert,' she reminded him. 'Hogmanay. You

haven't forgotten, surely? They're supposed to be your favourite band!'

'Er, no. No, course not. The Deceivers. Right . . .'

'Tom, are you okay?' She opened the door a little wider, concern etched on her face. 'I told you not to stay up all night reading that thing . . .' She was nodding towards the bedside cabinet. He looked and saw the Kindle lying open on top of it.

'I, I didn't,' he assured her. 'Really.'

'I hope not. Well, get yourself sorted anyway. Hamish is already raring to go! He wants to head into town early, so we can soak up the atmosphere.'

'Hamish?' Tom looked at her, remembering that the last time he saw his stepfather, he'd been in the act of mutating into some kind of monster. 'Is he . . . is he okay? I mean, has he . . . changed at all?'

'I'll say he has! He's like a big kid. He hasn't been to a pop concert in years. Me neither, come to think of it.'

'Are you sure it's still going ahead? The concert, I mean. What with the snow and everything, maybe . . .'

Now she really did look puzzled. 'Snow? What snow?'

'Oh, I thought . . .'

But she marched across the room and pulled open the curtains to reveal a sky that was surprisingly clear and bright. 'It's like a spring day,' she assured him. 'That's not something you get to say very often in Edinburgh. Even when it actually *is* spring!' She turned back and shook her head. 'Snow,' she said. 'Tom, sometimes I wonder what's going on in your head. Now, you'd better hit the shower. Your breakfast will be on the table in ten minutes. Be there or I'm giving it to the cat.' She went out again, closing the door behind her.

'Haven't even got a cat,' muttered Tom, but then reminded himself that in this version of his life there was every possibility that the family did have a cat, maybe even several of them. Possibly even a lion or a tiger. He started to get to his feet, but grunted when he felt a stab of pain in his right heel. He stared down for a moment then stripped off his socks to reveal feet that were filthy with a mixture of dried mud and blood. When he investigated the painful heel, he found a scab where the skin had recently been gashed. The socks were past all redemption, so he bundled them up and dropped them into the litterbin.

He limped out to the bathroom where he stripped off his clothes and got into the shower. The stream of hot water brought him fully awake and he spent quite some time soaping the cuts and scratches on his feet until they were clean. He dried himself, found a plaster in the medicine cabinet and taped it carefully over the injured heel. Back in his room he pulled clean clothes out of the wardrobe and a new pair of socks. When he examined the shoes he'd worn to climb Arthur's Seat, he decided that they too were ruined, so he slipped them into the bottom of his wardrobe and put on another pair of Converse that he'd brought with him. He was about to let himself out of the room when his gaze fell on the laptop on his desk and a sudden thought occurred to him. It had been stirred by something that Cat had asked him. 'What of that, Tom? In that museum of yours, I suppose it must have registered the year of my death?'

It occurred to him that right there on his laptop was a copy of Cat's novel, *The Path of Truth* which he had downloaded from Project Gutenberg. And he seemed to remember that there was also a little biography of Cat at the beginning of that book.

He couldn't help himself. A few moments later he'd booted up the laptop and was checking out the introduction. And there it was, right at the beginning of the novel. *Catriona McCallum 1813-1882.*

It hit him like a punch to the chest. He sat there staring open-mouthed at the screen as the horrible truth sank in. Back in Cat's time it was New Year's Eve, 1881. Which meant that in a matter of hours, she would be entering her final year on the planet. But what to do about it? Should he tell her? Warn her about it, so she could get her things in order, ready for departure? Or would it be kinder to say nothing, to let her blissfully carry on with the short time she had left? Suddenly, he wished he hadn't looked. It was a knowledge he really didn't want to have.

'Tom, come on, your food's getting cold!'

Mum's voice startled him. He got obediently to his feet, went out of the room and started down the staircase.

Halfway down, something weird happened. There was a sudden fluttering sound in Tom's head and the world around him seemed to grey out again. As he stood there, swaying uncertainly, the staircase began to change beneath him from the modest, carpeted steps of Hamish's place to the broad curve of the mahogany staircase in Cat's more spacious town house. Tom threw out a hand to the banister rail to steady himself and actually felt it remoulding itself beneath his grip. He stared around in astonishment. This was a new one!

Everything shimmered then settled and he was able to continue cautiously on his way, but now he was descending to the tiled floor of Cat's hallway. He made his way towards the drawing room where he knew he could generally find her. As he approached he heard voices talking within and when he opened the door and went inside, he found Cat sitting in an easy chair chatting to Lou who was sitting on the sofa opposite her, a silver tray of tea things on the table between them. They both looked up at Tom and smiled.

'Ah, Tom,' said Cat. 'I was just debating whether or not to give you a call. Mr Stevenson has dropped by with an invitation for us both.'

'An invitation?' Tom was trying to make sense of it all, but even to him, this sudden switching around in time and place was unusual, to say the least. He felt numbed, disorientated and as he looked at Cat, all he could think of was that she was going to die soon and there wasn't a thing he could do to prevent it.

'Yes.' Lou smiled at Tom. 'There's to be a musical recital in Princes Street Gardens, this afternoon,' he explained. 'In the Ross Bandstand. We're planning to go as a family and we thought that you and Mrs McCallum might care to accompany us. We'd be delighted if you'd accept.'

Tom struggled to get his head around this latest development. Wasn't the Deceiver's concert supposed to be happening in *exactly the same place*?

'Er, well, I suppose . . .'

'It's going to be splendid,' Lou assured him. 'A shame they couldn't have the event later on, to actually see in the New Year, but the city councillors thought that would be lacking in decorum.' He raised his eyebrows. 'So old-fashioned! But, they've had workmen clearing the snow all morning to make sure the event can go ahead. You will join us, won't you?'

'I haven't been to a music recital in years,' said Cat and as she said it, her face seemed to momentarily shimmer and change. For an instant, it looked decidedly like Mum's face.

'All the more reason to come with us,' said Lou and his face was shifting too, to look for a second or two like Hamish, before melting back again. Tom tried not to stare at him. 'You will come with us, won't you, Tom? Lloyd says it won't be the same without you.' He turned back to look at Cat. 'He's been telling us he has some big secret to unveil tonight, but he isn't going to say a word until we're all gathered in the park.' He laughed. 'Young boys, eh? Who can fathom what's going on in their heads?'

'Indeed,' said Cat, gravely and she looked at Tom. 'What do you say, Tom, do you feel up to going along?' She glanced at Lou. 'Tom's been feeling a little... under the weather,' she explained.

'Oh, well, all the more reason to get out in the fresh air. I'm sure if we all wrap up warm, it will be most invigorating.' Lou smiled at Tom. 'After your little performance on Christmas Eve, it's clear that you like music . . .'

'Well, yes,' admitted Tom. 'But . . .'

'Come and sit down,' Cat urged him. 'You're looking rather pale.'

'I'm feeling a bit odd,' Tom told them. But he came obediently around to the sofa and went to sit down beside Lou. As he lowered himself, the world shimmered and rippled and as his backside made contact with the sofa he registered that it felt curiously hard beneath him. Not like a sofa at all. More like a wooden chair . . .

'Toast?' asked Hamish.

Tom jolted in his seat and looked wildly around. He was sitting at the kitchen table in Fairmilehead and Mum and Hamish were looking at him oddly. Hamish was proffering a plate of buttered toast. Tom looked down at the table and saw a plate of bacon and eggs in front of him.

'What *is* this?' he asked the world in general.

'It's bacon and eggs,' said Mum, sounded crestfallen. 'I'm sorry, would you have preferred cereal? I thought a cooked breakfast would set us up for the day.'

'Er, no, no, that's fine. I didn't mean . . .'

Hamish coughed politely and Tom realised he was still holding out the plate of toast. Tom took a slice, even though the last thing he felt like doing now was eating. He dropped it onto his side plate and looked around the kitchen. Everything appeared to be perfectly ordinary. The clock on the wall registered the time as 10.48 and the second hand was moving in the right direction, which he supposed was *something* to be grateful for.

'Shocking, isn't it?' said Mum. 'Having breakfast this late in the day. It's more like brunch, really!' She forked a chunk of bacon into her mouth. 'Don't tell your father I let you lie in so late!'

'Catherine, the boy's on holiday,' said Hamish. 'When I was his age, I could sleep until the cows came home. I often did.' He winked at Tom. 'I'm guessing it's RLS keeping you up so late, eh?'

Tom stared at him. 'What do you mean?' he muttered.

'*Treasure Island*,' said Hamish. 'It's a fabulous book, isn't it? Where are you up to?'

'I'm, you know, I'm really not sure,' said Tom and was vaguely surprised to realise that this was absolutely true.

Hamish gave him a puzzled look. 'You're not sure?'

'Well, er, I think, er . . . it's the bit where they're all in the stockade,' elaborated Tom, citing the last part that he actually remembered reading. 'And they're waiting for the pirates to attack.'

'Splendid,' said Hamish. 'I've just finished rewriting that scene.'

Tom stared at him. 'You've . . . what?' he whispered.

Hamish's face was dissolving again, reshaping itself into Lou's leaner, more handsome features. At the same time the wooden chair under Tom's buttocks softened and he felt himself sinking down into the sofa. Tom tried not to panic. He wasn't sure what was going on but he didn't like it one little bit.

'I've been working like a demon,' said Lou. 'I think it's very nearly ready. And all thanks to you, Tom.' He reached out a hand and squeezed Tom's shoulder. 'In fact, there's something I wanted to show you.'

'Is everything all right, Tom?' interrupted Cat. 'You look a little confused.'

'No kidding?' muttered Tom. He shook his head, trying to dispel the dizziness that lingered there. 'I'm, I'm fine, really.'

Lou was reaching into the inside pocket of his jacket. He pulled out a sheet of writing paper and handed it to Tom. 'I thought I'd make my thanks a little more concrete,' he said. 'I hope you approve.'

Tom unfolded the sheet of paper and read the contents with a sinking heart. He had, of course, already seen this on his Kindle.

To Tom Afflick, an English gentleman, in accordance with whose classic taste the following narrative has been designed, it is now, in return for numerous delightful hours, and with the kindest wishes, dedicated by his affectionate friend, the author.

'What do you think?' asked Lou, brightly.

'I, I think . . . it really can't happen,' said Tom, quietly.

'I beg your pardon,' said Lou.

'This . . .' Tom waved the sheet of paper. 'I mean, don't get me wrong, it's dead nice of you and everything, it really is, but, you've got to change it.'

Lou looked exasperated. 'Change it? I thought you'd be pleased!'

'I am. Really, I am, but . . .' Tom was desperately trying to reason it out and then he seized on what he thought just might be his salvation. 'But, what about Lloyd?' he reasoned. 'What's he going to think?'

'Lloyd?' Lou reacted as though he was unfamiliar with the name. 'I really don't see what it has to do with him.'

'It's got *everything* to do with him. I mean, he'd go mental, wouldn't he? He'd go ballistic.'

Lou looked across to Cat as though seeking her help with the matter. Cat got up from her chair and came across to study the page in Tom's hand.

Lou was still trying to figure it out. 'You're saying that my stepson . . . would become mentally ill?' he asked.

'No. Not exactly. But he wouldn't be very pleased, would he? And who could blame him? After all, he was the one who started the whole thing. If he hadn't asked you to tell him a story about that map, there wouldn't *be* a *Treasure Island*, would there?' He looked up at Cat, seeking her support and thankfully, she took the hint.

'Tom's right, Mr Stevenson. Lloyd would surely feel cheated if this were allowed to stand. After all, he does think of himself as the story's inspiration.'

Lou frowned. 'I confess, I hadn't thought of it that way,' he admitted. He seemed to consider for a moment. 'Well, what if perhaps if I were to make it a joint dedication for the *two* of you?'

'No,' said Tom and even as he said it, he realised he was throwing away a real honour. The famous author of one of the world's best-loved books was offering to dedicate that book to him and he was throwing it back in the man's face! Part of him wanted to change his mind and accept, deal with the consequences later, but he knew he couldn't. 'No, it's a really cool idea, Lou, and thanks for the offer, but I reckon he'd still feel like I was pushing him out. It needs to be all about *him*.' He tried and failed to keep a note of irritation out of his voice. 'He'd love that.' He glanced at the paper again. 'The words you've got here, though, they're perfect. Just put his name there instead. And change "English gentleman" to "American gentleman". That'll be spot on.'

He handed the sheet of paper back to Lou, who looked somewhat deflated. 'Well, I must say, that's really not the reaction I was expecting, but now you have pointed it out to me, I can see the wisdom in your words. Lloyd is . . . a sensitive young soul.'

That's one name for him, thought Tom.

'And it's true, I suppose, that had it not been for him, we wouldn't be sitting here discussing the future publication of a book. So, I will reluctantly change the dedication. But Tom, I really would like to reward you for being such an inspiration to me. If there's anything I can do to show my appreciation, you only have to ask.'

'There is something,' said Tom.

'Yes?'

'I'd like you to look after Cat. When I'm gone.'

'You're going somewhere?'

'Er, yeah, soon, I think. I'm not really sure when,

but I get the feeling it won't be long now. But, when I go, I'd like you to keep an eye on my er . . . godmother. Make sure she doesn't come to any harm. Would you do that for me?'

'It would be my absolute pleasure,' said Lou. 'But I don't understand. You say you're going somewhere, but you're not entirely sure *when*?'

'It'll be when my mum and stepdad get back. From er, the South of France. I think they were talking about moving back to . . . to Manchester.'

'I see.' Lou frowned. 'Well, I'll be sorry to lose your company, Tom. Profoundly sorry.' He folded the piece of paper and slipped it back into his inside pocket. 'I have one or two things to attend to before the concert,' he announced. 'If you will both excuse me?' He got to his feet and headed towards the door. 'I'll see myself out,' he said. 'And I'll send a hansom for you at, shall we say one o'clock? We'll meet you by the main entrance to the park.'

'We shall look forward to it,' Cat assured him.

Lou bowed politely and went out, closing the door behind him. There was a brief silence while they waited for him to move out of earshot then Cat came and sat beside Tom on the sofa and took his hands in hers.

'What is going on?' she asked him. 'I've never seen you so unsettled.'

'I've been having these weird turns,' he told her. 'Slipping backwards and forwards in time. I can't seem to stop myself.'

'What do you mean?' said Mum's voice.

Cat's face was shimmering, dissolving. The seat beneath Tom hardened. Now it was Mum holding his hands and looking concerned. Tom glanced wildly around. There was no sign of Hamish.

'I mean, I mean, I . . .'

'What weird turns? Do you need to see a doctor?'

'No. No, of course not. I just . . . where's Hamish?'

Mum gave him an odd look. 'Didn't you hear him? He said he had a few jobs to do before we headed into town. Tom, you look awfully pale. Are you sure you're alright?'

'I'm fine, Mum.' Tom pulled his hands from hers. 'Stop fussing!'

'You didn't eat any breakfast,' observed Mum reproachfully, pointing at his virtually untouched plate. 'Would you like me to make you something else?'

He shook his head. 'I think . . . I think I might have a bit of a lie-down before we go out. Maybe you're right. Maybe I *did* stay up too late last night. Would that be okay?'

'Of course. You go on up,' she suggested. 'I'll give you a call when we're getting ready to leave.' She watched as he got unsteadily to his feet and went towards the door. 'I hope you're not coming down with something,' she said.

'I'm sure I'll be fine after I've had a rest,' Tom assured her. 'Really, you don't need to worry about me.'

He opened the door and stepped through it, only to find that there was no floor on the other side. Then he was falling into blackness once again, with the sound of wings beating all around him.

Eighteen

He came down hard, in a sitting position, with an impact that jarred the entire length of his spine. He shouted in pain and his arms slammed against two wooden surfaces. Almost instantly his wrists were encircled by cold metal cuffs that clamped themselves shut with an audible click. Likewise, his ankles were gripped and held in position. He tried to struggle and realised with a dull sense of shock that he was immobile, unable to move his body so much as an inch in any direction. Only his head was free.

His vision came slowly into focus and he stared helplessly around. He was in some kind of cellar, he decided: cold, damp and windowless, filled with the thick scents of earth and mould, lit only by a single oil lamp standing on a rickety wooden table to one side of him. He studied the table and his stomach twisted as he saw that various metal objects were set out in rows on its rough wooden surface – knives, pincers, hammers, even a couple of rusty-looking saws. He didn't want to think about what they might be used for.

He tried again to struggle against the bonds that held him, but when he focused his attention on them, he saw that the cuffs were securely anchored into the wooden arm rests. As his confusion subsided, a nagging fear began to grow in the pit of his stomach. Where was he? Why was he here in this unfamiliar place? Just then a voice spoke from a short distance away and terror engulfed him. It was a horribly familiar voice – coarse, rasping, pitiless.

'So, Tom, here we are, at last. Just the two of us. I was beginning to think this day would never come.'

A cloaked figure stepped silently out of the shadows. The beaked mask had been removed and was clutched in one gloved hand. The animated, skull-like face was terrible to behold. McSweeny came to a halt beside the table, his sightless eye sockets gazing at Tom with a strange and terrible intensity. 'I got tired of chasing you,' he said, as if by way of explanation. 'Decided it was time you came to me. So much less effort on my part.'

'You . . . you'd better let me go,' gasped Tom. He was so scared he could hardly breathe. 'Let me go or I'll–'

'You'll what, Tom? What will you do? What can you hope to do to me that you haven't done already?' McSweeny lifted his free hand to gesture at his exposed skull. 'Look at your handiwork, Tom. Are you proud of it?'

Tom shook his head. 'That's . . . that's not my fault,' he insisted. 'You kept coming after me. You wouldn't give up. I didn't mean for that to happen. You fell and I didn't even know what was in that barrel!'

'Is that a fact? But it happened just the same, Tom, and as I'm sure you'll appreciate, I'm far from happy about it.' He pointed to something standing on the table, a small wooden cask. 'Do you know what's in that, Tom? Do you?'

Tom shook his head.

'It's quicklime. I thought perhaps I might return the favour.'

'No!' Tom tried again to struggle against his bonds, but it was no use. 'No, you . . . you can't!'

'Oh, but I *can*. You see, I can do whatever I've a mind to. You're my prisoner. I can do exactly as I like and I can take my own sweet time about it.' He reached out to the table and brushed his gloved fingers along the line of lethal-looking instruments. 'I could practice my surgery skills, perhaps? Been a while since I was called upon to demonstrate them. You remember the procedures we did in Mary King's Close, Tom? How I made you help me with them? How about we make you the patient instead? We could see how much pain you're able to take before you start begging me to finish you off.'

Tom looked frantically around the room. 'Where *is* this place?' he cried.

'It's somewhere of my own making,' McSweeny told him. 'A place between worlds. A place where nobody will hear you scream.' He laughed unpleasantly and picked up a pair of pincers. He made a couple of snipping motions on the air. 'A bit of dentistry perhaps?' he murmured. 'Are your teeth in good order, Tom? Do you think we should check?'

But he made no move to come any closer. A vague suspicion flowered at the back of Tom's mind. He made a valiant effort to calm himself and stared defiantly back at his captor. 'It . . . it isn't real, is it?' he said. 'This place. Any of it. It's just stuff you've made me *see*. Because you're in my head. All of this is in my head.'

McSweeny chuckled. 'Oh, is that the best you can do?' he said. 'Keep telling yourself that, Tom. It's not real. It's all in your head! It might help you to handle the pain.' He took a threatening step closer, but still made no real attempt to attack which made Tom begin to think that he might be on to something.

'That's it, isn't it? That's why . . . that's why you've never quite managed to get hold of me. Not since Mary King's Close. Because you're out of your own time. You're like – you're like a bad dream. You're in my head, but that's *all* you are.'

'Think so, Tom?' McSweeny sniggered. 'Better try telling that to the wee girl. What was her name? Morag? Sweet little thing. Do you think *she* was convinced that I was real?'

'Yes, but . . . but you *were* real then.'

'And I'm real now. And quite capable of inflicting pain on you, my boy.'

'Then why are you just talking about it? Why don't you do something? Go on, let's see what you can do.'

There was a long silence. The skull face continued to stare at Tom with evident hatred, but he sensed indecision. He really had hit on something here. And when he thought about it, it explained so much. All those near misses. All those times that McSweeny's blade hadn't quite hit its target. Even that last incident, when Tom and Lloyd had leapt from the hansom cab, seconds before it went into the river. It was as though McSweeny was haunting him, inflicting terror and worry, but not actually able to physically injure him.

'I think that's it,' murmured Tom. 'I can make changes because *I'm* still alive. But you died in 1645.'

McSweeny found his voice. 'Shall I tell you what I'm going to do, Tom? Instead of hurting you directly, I'll go after the new one. What does this one call herself? Oh yes, Catriona. Such a tragic turn of events! She was your sweetheart for a while, back in the day, wasn't she? And now, she's a lonely old woman, eking out her last months of life. Oh, and that hurts you, Tom, doesn't it? It's been exquisite experiencing your pain over the last few days.'

Tom glared at him. 'Whatever you say, I killed you. I *know* I did. When we fell through that roof in Mary King's Close, the knife went into your heart and you died. But now, you're like . . . you're like a ghost. How else do you follow me through time? It's like you slip between the cracks in the pavement. And you've made this place out of your own mind, haven't you? Which means that I can *un*make it.'

Tom stared at his left wrist and concentrated hard.

'What are you trying to do?' mocked McSweeny. 'You honestly think that's going to make any difference?'

Tom continued to stare at the cuff, but still nothing happened.

'You little fool! You really believe you can change things?' There was a hint of desperation in McSweeny's voice now and that gave Tom the power to continue. He deepened his concentration, imagined his wrist being unshackled and now, somehow, he could feel that it was actually beginning to work. As he stared at the metal cuff, it shimmered, faded, disappeared. His left hand was suddenly free and he was able to lift it to show McSweeny, who was looking at him now in evident dismay.

'There,' said Tom. '*That's* how real all this is.' The knowledge gave him more strength. He concentrated again, allowed his mind to travel outwards and this time it was much easier. His right hand and his ankles were free also. He got up out of the chair, while McSweeny stood there, clearly unsure of what to do. 'Now what's left for you?' he asked McSweeny. 'You're beaten. I know what you are. I know how to deal with you.'

McSweeny's lips curved into a mirthless smile. 'But Catriona doesn't know that, does she?' he said. And he began to fade.

'No, wait!' Tom lunged forward and tried to throw his arms around McSweeny, but the man's bony body seemed to dissolve like smoke and was gone. Tom hurtled forward towards the stone floor, but that too melted away before him and once again, he was falling, spinning, his head filled with a giddy red nausea

Nineteen

He came down hard, once again, in a sitting position and slumped back with a gasp against soft leather. Sweat was running down his face and the world was swaying and shuddering. It took him a little while to realise that he was, once again, in the interior of a hansom cab. Opposite him, he saw Cat, looking at him with obvious concern.

'Where did you go to?' she asked him quietly.

'I disappeared?' he asked her.

'Only momentarily. You became transparent. I could see right through you. I thought you were leaving me again, but then you came back. Did you return to your own time?'

'You don't want to know where I went,' he told her. He shook the last traces of dizziness out of his head and pulled aside the window blind to peep out. The unexpected blaze of bright sunshine made him squint. He saw that the cab was moving along Princes Street, which was thronged with hundreds of people, all dressed in their winter clothes, moving restlessly to and fro along the pavements. The snow had melted away in the unexpected sunshine, leaving only stubborn clusters of ice here and there. Vendors were shouting their wares from stalls set up along the route and there was an air of high excitement. Tom reminded himself that it was New Year's Eve.

'So we're off to meet the Stevensons?' he ventured. 'For the concert?'

Cat nodded. She looked tired, Tom thought, her eyes ringed with red as though she was in need of sleep. 'We're almost there,' she said and that somehow reminded Tom that they were only hours away from 1882 – the year in which Cat was destined to die. Once again he felt torn. Should he tell her what he knew, so that she could prepare herself? Or was it better to leave her in blissful ignorance? He had a terrible sense of foreboding and began to wish that they had stayed at home.

'Cat,' he said. 'There's something I have to tell you. It's really important.'

She leaned forward, intrigued. 'Go on,' she said.

'You remember I told you about McSweeny? The man from Mary King's Close.'

She nodded. 'The plague doctor,' she said. 'Yes, I've seen him.'

Tom narrowed his eyes for a moment, confused and then remembered that Cat *had* seen him briefly on Arthur's Seat, had even been chased by him for a short distance. 'Oh, yes,' he said. 'I forgot. Well, I've just realised something about him. Something important.'

'Yes?'

'He . . . he's not real, Cat. He's a ghost.'

Cat frowned. 'The man I saw seemed real enough,' she said.

'Yes, I know he *looks* real. But if he should come for you, you must remember that he can't harm you. He's just a . . . a shadow.'

She seemed to consider this for a moment. 'I'll try to remember that,' she said. 'Do you have any reason to believe that we *will* see him again?'

'I think . . .' He was reluctant to tell her, but then decided that he had to. 'I think he might try to get to you, Cat. To frighten you, because he knows that would cause me pain and I think he knows that's all he can do to me now.' Tom shook his head. 'It's crazy. I've spent so much time running away from him, scared out of my wits, but if I'd just stood my ground when he came back after I killed him, the first time.'

Catriona looked concerned at this. 'You're saying you killed somebody?'

'Oh, not on purpose! We were fighting. This was back in 1645 when I first knew him, when he was human. We fell through a skylight and he was carrying a knife.' For a moment, Tom was actually back there, running madly for his life across the rooftops of Mary King's Close. He made an effort to shut the images out of his head. 'I didn't understand how he could chase me through time like he does. But now, I think I get it. And you know what? I'm beginning to think that I might be able to do it too. I just need to learn how to control it.'

The coachman shouted, 'Whoah,' and the cab

lurched to a halt. The door swung open and there was Lou, smiling at them. 'Right on time,' he said. 'A warm welcome to you both.' He reached in to take Cat's hand and helped her to climb out of the cab. Tom jumped down after her to see Fran and Lloyd standing a short distance away, by the park gates, both of them wrapped up in warm clothing. 'We're in good time for the performance,' Lou assured Cat. He offered her his arm and gave the other to Fran, then led the way towards the entrance and down the long flight of stone steps which were crowded with throngs of people. Tom found himself walking alongside Lloyd. The boy had that sly look about him that Tom had already come to detest.

'I'm really looking forward to this,' said Lloyd, quietly. He was wearing a heavy overcoat, a tartan scarf and a cloth cap and he looked somehow much stouter than he actually was.

'The concert?' muttered Tom, although he already knew that Lloyd hadn't meant that.

'No. I'm talking about the moment when I expose you,' Lloyd corrected him, smiling maliciously.

'Why would you do that?' Tom asked him. 'I thought I told you, if you want your dad to be a famous writer, then . . .'

'But he's already done the rewrites,' interrupted Lloyd. 'So it can't make any difference now, can it?'

'It's not as simple as that,' Tom assured him. 'You remember what I said about the dominoes? You pull one piece out and . . .'

'I can't wait to see Papa's face,' interrupted Lloyd.

'When he finds out that you're from the future he won't think quite so highly of you then, will he?'

Tom shrugged, thought about it for a moment. 'I think he'll be thrilled,' he said.

Lloyd looked puzzled. 'Huh?' he muttered.

'He'll be mad for it, won't he? He'll probably think I'm the most amazing person he's ever met.'

Lloyd looked doubtful. 'No, no he won't. He'll think you're an imposter,' he insisted. 'He'll feel like you've cheated him.'

'I don't see it that way. I reckon he'll want to know all about me. You know what? He'll probably want to write a whole book about my adventures. Yeah, maybe that'll be the book that makes him famous. *The Adventures of Tom Afflick – Time Traveller*.

Lloyd's expression was priceless. He looked as though somebody was holding a rotten egg under his nose. He slowed to a halt. 'You're just saying that,' he protested. 'I think he'll tell you to leave.'

'Well, let's put it to the test, shall we?' said Tom, coolly. He pointed to Lou walking up ahead. 'Tell him,' he suggested.

'I will too,' said Lloyd. 'Don't think I won't.'

'Go on, then. Be my guest.'

But Lloyd made no attempt to catch up with his stepfather. He gritted his teeth and scowled. 'I hate you,' he said.

'Hey, come on, don't lag behind!' The voice made Tom glance up in surprise, because it didn't sound anything like Lou. And as he looked up, everything around Tom shimmered, rippled and went suddenly, abruptly dark. The man up ahead was Hamish, dressed in a heavy overcoat and a hat with woolly earflaps. The woman on his arm, wearing a thick quilted jacket, was Mum. Tom looked around and realised that Lloyd had vanished and now he was standing on an even more crowded staircase. All around him, people dressed in modern clothing were pushing and jostling good-naturedly, many of them swigging alcohol from cans of beer and cider. Below them, the park was lit up by what looked like thousands of fairy lights and loud music filled the air.

'Come on, slow coach,' shouted Mum.

Tom quickened his pace and pushed his way down the last few steps. As he approached his companions, Hamish handed him a brightly coloured paper ticket. 'Just in case we get split up,' he shouted over the sonic roar of the music. He looked around in evident delight. 'How about this?' he bellowed. 'The papers said there's eighty thousand people out on the streets tonight! Imagine that!'

Tom gazed blankly around. He didn't have to imagine it. It was all around him.

'Where did you disappear to?' Mum asked him.

Tom could only shrug his shoulders. 'Er, I was talking to someone,' he muttered. 'Over there.' He waved a hand in a general direction.

'A stranger?' Mum's expression registered disapproval. 'Well stay close, we don't want to get separated in this crowd,' she said.

'Come on,' said Hamish. 'Your band is due to hit the stage any minute.'

They continued on through the press of bodies. It seemed inconceivable that so many people could manage to crush themselves into such a modest space. Up ahead they could see the brilliant lights of the stage and when they finally jostled their way closer, they came to a narrow gateway guarded by two security men. They had to show their tickets to go through the gates onto the steps of the Ross Bandstand. 'I got us VIP tickets,' Hamish told them, beaming proudly as he led them into the smaller crowd beyond. 'It was only another twenty notes.' He waved at the much bigger crowd ranged up the hillside behind them. 'We'll have a better view than that lot.'

They edged through the rows of people ranged on the steps until they were standing right in front of the huge stage. As they settled themselves in, Tom saw that a DJ was hunched over a turntable in its very centre, pumping out an ear-splitting mix of sound, making the people in the crowd below him twitch and jerk like demented marionettes. He was drenched in floods of coloured light, changing and shifting in time to the music and clouds of dry ice swirled and billowed around him.

'I don't care for this house stuff,' bellowed Hamish. 'Bring on the live music, I say.' He had produced a can of Tennents lager from the pocket of his coat and was taking liberal swigs from it. Clearly, even the new, more temperate Hamish drew the line at drinking diet Coke on New Year's Eve. He offered Tom a swig from the can but Tom shook his head. He was feeling mixed-up enough right now without adding to the problem.

The music emanating from the stage came to a sudden, abrupt halt and the DJ raised one hand in the air.

Tom squinted as sunlight blazed into his eyes again. As he stared in disbelief, the Ross Bandstand reshaped itself into a small round construction of cast iron with a tin roof. The DJ shimmered, rippled and turned into a portly, bearded gentleman wearing a navy blue uniform and a peaked hat. He was holding a conductor's baton. Around him sat the various uniformed members of a brass band, their gleaming instruments reflecting the winter sunlight. The conductor raised the baton and waited for complete silence. Then he brought it down again and the band launched into a jaunty rendition of *Onward Christian Soldiers*.

'No freakin' way!' gasped Tom and his companions all turned to look at him in surprise.

He coughed in an attempt to hide his embarrassment. Cat gave him a look that said 'Is everything alright?' He gave her a reassuring smile, but in truth, things weren't even close to normal. He felt as though everything was slipping out of control, like he was on a runaway train, unable to slow it down.

'They're very good, aren't they?' said Lou, who was tapping his foot politely to the beat, but Tom couldn't help feeling that this music was a bit tame for his taste. He looked around the crowd and noticed for the first time that every single person he could see, male or female, was wearing a hat of some kind. He realised that he was almost certainly the only bareheaded person in the park.

The brass band hit the final chord and the audience responded with enthusiastic applause. The conductor turned to face the crowd and bowed his head. He waited until the clapping had died away and then opened his mouth to speak.

'Good evening, Edinburgh!' he bellowed, his voice suddenly amplified to an echoing scream. 'Are you ready to rock?'

Night fell in an instant, as though somebody had switched off the sun and around Tom, an appreciative roar went up from the crowd. The conductor was the DJ again, leaning in to a microphone to deliver his introduction.

'Will you give a great big Edinburgh welcome to the best rock and roll band on the planet? Ladies and gentlemen . . . it's The Deceivers!'

And the band were striding out on stage as thousands of cameras, held aloft, flashed a flickering, dazzling welcome. Chris Spencer, the drummer, slipped in behind a drum kit the size of a tank and launched into a four-four rhythm. Tom could feel the sound of the bass drum thudding in his chest like an amplified heartbeat. Steve Lampton, the bass player, took up his position to stage left and added an urgent, throbbing bass line. Adrian Langan, skinny and bespectacled, slid in behind a stack of state-of-the-art keyboards and began to layer slabs of brooding chords over the rhythm and then lead guitarist, Scott Griffin, plugged in his guitar and came in with a strident, sinewy riff. The crowd recognised the tune and a cheer went up, followed by an even bigger roar of approval, as singer/guitarist Jenny Slade strode out onto the stage, dressed in her trademark outfit of blue jeans and black leather jacket. She stepped up to the microphone, grinned down at the crowd below her and said, 'Hello, Edinburgh. Are you ready to party?'

The screams that came up from the crowd announced that they were indeed ready to do exactly that.

'Okay. This one's called *Time Traveller*.'

This wasn't a surprise to Tom. It was a recent hit record, a top ten single and Tom supposed it was what had attracted him to the band in the first place. When he'd first heard the song on the radio, it felt as though the lyrics had been written especially with him in mind.

> *I'm a time traveller baby, slipping through the years.*
> *Said goodbye to sorrow, kissed away my fears.*
> *Go wherever fate will take me. Don't ever have a say.*
> *Won't let the future break me. I'll live to love another day.*
> *When I feel the past is calling.*
> *When I feel that I am falling.*
> *Just say goodbye to the present. Live to love another day.*

Mum leaned in close. 'They're great, aren't they?' she yelled into Tom's ear. He nodded, but he couldn't settle to enjoy the music. He was waiting for the next time-shift to hit him. Annoyingly, it happened just as

Scott Griffin went into the guitar solo. One moment Scott was unleashing a shrill barrage of screaming, gut-rending sound into the audience. The next, the music dropped in volume and turned into a polite, plodding hymn, but for a moment Tom could still see The Deceivers up there, seemingly crammed into the tiny bandstand and turning out the kind of music they wouldn't have even known how to play. Then everything shimmered, rippled and once again it was daytime and the brass band was playing, the performers still and expressionless in their seats as they cradled their instruments.

'I do love a good brass band,' announced Lou and Tom turned his head to look. He registered with a dull sense of shock that Fran was standing to one side of Lou and Lloyd was on the other. But there was no sign of Cat anywhere.

'Where is she?' he yelled and once again, heads turned to look in his direction. 'Where's Cat?'

Lou smiled. 'Did you not see? She went with the entertainer. The man in fancy dress? He asked her to help him with an illusion.' He pointed back into the thick of the crowd and Tom saw two figures moving away from him. Cat was now walking arm-in-arm with a tall figure, a man dressed in a long leather cloak and a strange beak-like mask.

'No!' whispered Tom. 'Why did you let him take her?' He turned and began to push his way back through the crowd.

'Tom, where are you going?' called Fran. 'He promised to escort her back in a few minutes.'

Tom ignored her. He weaved his way through the ranks of bodies, intent on catching up with the two people ahead of him. But he'd only taken a few steps when everything went dark again.

Twenty

It was Hogmanay night and the crowd had mutated into a swaying, dancing, chanting press of drunken people, and somehow Tom could still see Cat and McSweeny, gliding through the throngs ahead of him, as though they no longer had any real substance.

Tom quickened his pace, but he was still entirely solid and had to shoulder his way through the audience. The world around him kept fading and flickering like a dodgy light fitting. For an instant it was full daylight again and the crowd were polite, well dressed people in nineteenth century clothing, staring at him indignantly as he jostled his way through their midst; the next, it was pitch dark and everyone around him wore hoodies and anoraks and some of them were far from polite when he bumped into them. The air smelled of beer and cigarettes and the music continued to pump out, one moment reserved and plodding, the next a head-splitting grind of heavy rock. Tom felt disorientated by it all, but he gritted his teeth and kept going.

Cat and McSweeny had emerged on the far side of the

crowd as daylight dawned once more and they hurried along the path to the entrance. Cat seemed to have no fear of her companion, she was striding alongside him as though in some kind of trance and Tom saw that McSweeny had an arm draped around her shoulders, as though claiming her as his property. Finally, Tom too emerged from the midst of the shifting, changing crowd and began to run after the two figures, just as darkness descended once again. The sound of the band diminished a little as he began to catch them up, but Cat and McSweeny were halfway up the staircase to the entrance before he finally closed on them. The stairs were deserted now, everyone's attention focused on the band.

'Wait!' he yelled and started up the steps.

McSweeny came to a halt and spun around to face him. He lifted his free hand and pulled the mask aside, revealing that hideous face. Cat didn't react to it. She was looking straight ahead, her expression blank. It was obvious now that she really was in some kind of trance.

'Tom,' said McSweeny. 'You are persistent, I must give you that.'

'Let her go,' said Tom. He began to climb cautiously closer, taking it one step at a time. 'Please. This isn't about her. It's between us. You and me.'

'Do you think so?' The man's exposed teeth clacked together in a rictus grin. 'But Tom, I thought I explained. Anything I can do to inflict pain on you gives me the most intense pleasure. And this lady . . .' He traced a gloved hand down the side of Cat's face.

'This lady is very special to you, isn't she, Tom? Oh, yes. She was your sweetheart once upon a time and now . . . now she's your closest friend. Which is why she has to die.'

'No. You can't hurt her.' Tom licked his lips. 'Cat, listen to me. He can't hurt you. He's just a . . . a bad memory.'

'Keep talking, Tom,' rasped McSweeny. 'It's music to my ears.'

'Cat, can you hear me? Please listen. He can't kill you. Shall I tell you how I know that? Because . . . because it's not your time to die. I know when that is, I've seen it written down. And he can't change that. He just can't.'

McSweeny laughed derisively. 'I know only too well when she dies, Tom. In 1882. Which by my reckoning, is in about two minutes time.'

Tom stared at McSweeny in dismay. He hadn't realised how late it was. He reached into his pocket and pulled out the watch, the one that Cat had given him. He flipped it open and saw that McSweeny was right.

'The dates you saw written down,' murmured McSweeny. 'I'm not arguing with them. But I doubt that they mentioned how *far* into 1882 it actually was.'

'Even so.' Tom pushed the watch back into his pocket and climbed up another step. 'Even so, you . . . you can't hurt her. I won't let you.'

'My dear Tom, what makes you think you can stop me?'

Over on the stage the music came to an abrupt halt

and Tom heard Jenny Slade's voice calling out over the PA system. 'Are you ready, Edinburgh? There's just two minutes to go!'

A metal blade seemed to sprout from McSweeny's gloved hand as if by magic. 'If there's something you'd like to say to Catriona,' he murmured. 'Now would seem like a good time.'

Tom shook his head. He couldn't . . . *wouldn't* allow this to happen.

'Cat,' he said. 'Cat, listen to me!'

Her eyes seemed to widen a little, her head shifted slightly to the right. Now she was looking directly at him. Encouraged, he took another step closer.

'I wish, I wish I could have stayed with you in 1829. It felt right being with you. It felt like we belonged together.' The ghost of a smile played on Cat's lips, as if she was remembering something. 'What if I told you I thought we could go back there. The two of us. So we could be together again?'

'Oh, so now who's trying to change history,' sneered McSweeny. 'You can't do that, Tom, don't even pretend that you can.'

'I'm not pretending,' said Tom. 'I really think I can do it.'

'Don't you understand? Haven't you caught on yet? Time doesn't exist, Tom. It's a concept created by man. There are no rules, none of it makes any sense. You might think you've got the measure of it, but that's just when it will leap up like a mad dog and bite you!'

From the stage, Jenny's voice cut through the silence. 'One minute to go, Edinburgh!' Cheers rippled out from the crowd. Anticipation was mounting.

Tom held out a hand and took a step closer. 'All we have to do, Cat, is hang on tight to each other. And we can do that, can't we? You remember how I brought you back with me that time? Well, we could move in the other direction. I'm sure of it.'

McSweeny was moving his head from side-to-side, his neck bones making a strange creaking sound. 'Empty words,' he jeered. 'Empty promises. From the boy with everything to lose.'

'No. No, I think . . . I think I know how to do it, Cat! Let me show you how. Please.'

'Twenty seconds, Edinburgh! Will you count with me? Nineteen, eighteen, seventeen, sixteen . . .' Yells of anticipation from the crowd as the old year leaned dangerously towards the new one.

McSweeny's hand moved a fraction. The blade glittered malevolently beside Cat's throat. 'Say goodbye to her, Tom. It's your last chance.'

It was now or never. Tom concentrated really hard and willed himself to make something happen. He knew he didn't have to go back far. Just a few moments and a few short steps. The world shimmered and rippled around him, he felt the stone steps melting under his feet and he was gone, slipping through the cracks in time. Almost instantly the world solidified again and he was standing on the steps, directly behind McSweeny and Cat. He twisted around as he heard Jenny Slade yell, 'One minute to go Edinburgh!'

He didn't hesitate. He grabbed McSweeny's wrist in one hand and pulled it away from Cat's neck. Then with the other hand, as hard as he could, he punched the side of McSweeny's head and sent him flailing down the steps in a tangle of bone and leather. He grabbed Cat and shook her awake. 'Get back up to the gates,' he yelled at her. 'Cat, move yourself! Now!'

She gazed at him blankly, a sleeper rudely awoken, but she obeyed him instinctively, moving up towards the entrance gates. Tom turned back to see McSweeny lying in a sprawl at the bottom of the steps. He was recovering himself. He glared upwards and dull red lights seemed to glow in his empty eye sockets.

'You slippery little swine,' he growled.

He got to his feet, retrieved the knife from where it had fallen and started back up, his gaze fixed not on Tom, but on Cat, who was waiting now, beside the gates. Tom saw his enemy's intention and ran down the steps just as McSweeny began to fade away. Tom leapt, threw his arms around the man's bony frame and clung on tight as the two of them went hurtling headlong into a blizzard of sound and light. The world was a spinning maelstrom but Tom wasn't going to let go this time. He managed to release his right arm and launched punch after punch at that hated, skull-like face, putting all the force he could muster into each blow. The face came apart beneath the onslaught, shattering into white splinters and flying off in all directions. McSweeny went spinning away with a yell of terror, falling to bits as he tumbled.

And then, abruptly, Tom was alone. He made contact with hard stone and went tumbling, rolling over and over down the steps, pain hammering through his body with such force that it snatched his breath away.

He came to a halt and gazed up the steps to see Cat, looking down at him in horror.

'Tom!' she gasped.

He was aware of a warm wetness on his chest. He put his hand to it and the fingers came away soaked in blood.

Jenny Slade's voice was booming in his ears.

'Ten, nine, eight, seven . . .'

He clung grimly onto consciousness as Cat started down the steps towards him, one hand outstretched.

'Six, five, four, three, two, ONE!'

And then the world seemed to explode in a roar of sound and fury and Cat's anxious face was lit by a bright red glow. Tom twisted his head to look towards the silhouette of the castle, high above them, and he realised it was fireworks, an incredible display of them, bursting out of the building on columns of fire and smoke like some futuristic war, illuminating the night sky with their brilliance. The steps seemed to shake and shudder beneath him as giant rockets bloomed in the heavens like gigantic, exotic flowers. At a different time he would have watched in open-mouthed awe, but a terrible pain was spilling through his guts. He felt as though he'd been torn in half and he knew in that moment that he was dying, that he was more badly injured than a fall down a flight of steps could possibly have caused. The injustice of it made him gasp and his eyes filled with hot tears.

Cat got down the steps and knelt beside him. 'Tom,' she gasped. 'Tom, what's happened to you? You're bleeding.'

'I, I don't know. I think . . .' But even as he spoke, Cat seemed to be moving away from him, she seemed to be gliding along a dark corridor into the distance and though he shouted out her name again and again, he realised that she could no longer hear him. He was heading somewhere beyond her reach. The world breathed out, a great mournful sigh of discontent and he went down, one last time, into the darkness.

Twenty-One

He was hanging upside down in the dark and there was a stench of petrol in his nostrils, the mournful wailing of sirens in his ears, and when he managed to open his eyes he was dimly aware of flashing lights coming from somewhere outside. But outside where? He looked around, blinking with the effort, and realised he was inside Hamish's overturned car. Below him, on the roof, he could see his Kindle lying there, still illuminated at the page he had been reading. As he looked at it, red spots splattered down onto the screen and he realised that it was blood. His blood. Then the pain hit him, unbelievable pain, rippling through his chest and stomach and making him gasp for breath.

Hands groped for him and then two men in fluorescent jackets were gently unstrapping him from the seat belt, they were easing him out through a shattered open doorway into a chaos of moving vehicles and flashing lights. They lifted him onto some kind of stretcher and when he looked down at himself, he was shocked to see that his shirt was absolutely soaked with blood.

He heard somebody screaming. It seemed a long way off but when he turned his head to one side, he saw Mum, struggling to get to him. She was shouting his name and there was blood on her face. Hamish and another man in a yellow jacket were holding her back, telling her to let the professionals deal with it. She was fighting them, trying to push them away but they held onto her. Hamish had tears in his eyes and it occurred to Tom that he had never seen the man cry before. He told himself that maybe old Hamish wasn't so bad, after all.

Tom was sure of one thing. This was no alternative reality. This was actually happening. He tried to speak, to tell Mum not to cry, that he was okay, but when he opened his mouth he found he didn't have the strength to make a sound and that was when he knew how serious it really was.

He was being lifted now, into the warm glow of light, and he realised that he was in an ambulance. There was a sliding sensation beneath him and something clicked firmly into position. A rubbery mask was clamped down over his mouth and he felt a rush of icy air flooding into his lungs, but he was still having difficulty drawing breath. He was dimly aware of his shirt being opened, gloved hands touching him, applying sticky things to his chest, things that he couldn't quite see. There was the sound of an engine and the ambulance lurched into motion. A few seconds later he heard the sound of a siren, a long lonely wail. Then he heard more sobbing and realised that Mum and Hamish were in the ambulance, over by the doors, but they were being kept back by a grim-faced man, while a young woman in a green uniform attended to Tom. Her face was kind but grave and he could see in her eyes that she was concerned.

'You're OK, Tom,' she told him, though her voice seemed somehow very distant. 'You've been involved in a traffic accident and we're taking you to the hospital. Stay with me, now. Do you hear? You must try and stay with me.'

But he didn't feel inclined to do that. He was tired, so very tired. Instead, with some difficulty, he slid a hand down into the pocket of his coat and felt the reassuring touch of cold metal against his fingertips. He took the pocket watch out and held it up where he could see it. He flipped it open. It was proof, he thought sadly, the final proof he had always wanted.

'Now, now, we don't need that,' said the woman, and tried to take it from him, but he brushed her hands away. He looked past her to his mum, sobbing in Hamish's arms, and tried to give her a reassuring smile, but he realised she wouldn't see it behind the mask. He knew what he had to do now and he thought he had finally mastered the way to make it happen. As he looked at Mum, he noticed one last detail. Perched on a metal rail on one side of the ambulance sat a magpie, its head tilted to one side. It was watching him intently. Nobody else in the ambulance seemed to be aware of it.

Tom concentrated on the watch, concentrated all that was left of his conscious mind. And as he stared at its face, something weird happened. The hands of the watch started to go backwards. He almost laughed, but he didn't have the strength for that. He knew it was working. Then the things he wanted to happen began to happen. He felt the stretcher beneath him turning soft and insubstantial. He heard the ambulance woman's incredulous cry, mingled with the soft beat of the magpie's wings as they blurred into motion. And he finally understood why the bird was there, why it had been there from the very beginning. It was his guide. It was there to bring him home.

Then the ambulance was gone and he was drifting downwards, weightless, like an autumn leaf falling in the night. The black and white wings beat rhythmically above him, lulling him, calming him. He seemed to fall for a very long time, but that didn't surprise him, because he knew that he had a long way to go.

When his feet finally thumped against boggy ground, he knew exactly where he was. He was still holding the watch. It had come with him, because it was touching him and it had somehow survived the journey, even though it hadn't been created yet. The hands were still now, because he had come to a halt and he was right where he wanted to be. It was just a little after two o clock in the afternoon. He took a moment to gather his thoughts. He looked down at his open shirt, concerned that maybe the injuries had travelled with him too, but he was relieved to see there were no wounds on his chest, just the little red marks where monitors had been stuck to his skin. What was it McSweeny had said to him on the park steps?

'Don't you understand. Haven't you caught on,

yet? Time doesn't exist. It's a concept created by man. There are no rules, none of it makes any sense.'

That might be true, but he knew where he was now and it was exactly where and when he wanted to be. And this time, he told himself, this time he was here to stay. It was very cold and he quickly buttoned up his shirt and shrugged his winter coat tighter around him.

Then he turned his head to look downhill and she was exactly where he'd expected her to be, just as he'd pictured her in his head before he set off. She was cloaked and bonneted and she was walking away from him, descending the hill, her head bowed in evident sorrow. He grinned and relished the moment for a few seconds. He wasn't worried about a thing. He knew now that he had all the time in the world to spend with her. When he felt ready, he cupped his hands to his mouth and shouted her name.

It echoed across the hillside.

She stopped. She turned. Even at this distance he could see the smile of delight on her face as she lifted a hand to wave at him.

Titles in this series